the
Sins of
a good *Wife*

SHERRY BERRY

The Sins of a Good Wife

Copyright ©2018 Sherry Adams

Cover and Interior Design
DHBonner Virtual Solutions, LLC
www.dhbonner.net

ISBN-13:9781986543569

Printed in the USA

This book is **dedicated** to
my mom and my dad, Shadie and William,

my siblings Michael, Shirley and Terry,

and my niece, Shenetha.

I know that you would be

really proud and I wish I could

share this moment

with you all.

August 10, 2015

∗ ∗ ∗

Chassidy was all cried out. The past three years had been marked by an endless stream of tears. On the surface she had it all— handsome husband, beautiful daughter, good-paying job, home, car, and money saved. For the first time ever, she had less bills than income and could afford to take island vacations or splurge on some of the things she wanted. Things should have been great, but they weren't.

Coming home from work each day to face Eric and the life that came along with him made her feel like she was trapped in a room that lacked oxygen. She gasped for air, but breathing was increasingly difficult when he was near her. He was cold and unloving, the complete opposite of what she had imagined for herself when she played make-believe as a child. He was no Prince Charming or Knight in shining armor and he made it a point to show her how much he loathed her every day with his words and actions. But still a part of her hoped things would get better.

Of the things on her list of having it all, the only one that had brought any semblance of joy was her precious three-year-old daughter, Serenity. Serenity was God's gift to her. She never went through the "terrible two's or three's." She was just a wonderful child who gave the most passionate hugs and kisses— Serenity was the personification of love. Yet, her love couldn't compensate for the hole in Chassidy's heart. On the inside, at the very core of who Chassidy was, something very important was missing.

Truth be told, Serenity was the glue that held their marriage together. She was the main reason Chassidy and Eric chose to get married and try to make things work when Chassidy found out she was pregnant. Had it not been for Serenity, Chassidy would have never pursued a real relationship or marriage with a man she abhorred as much as she did Eric. But her hopes for a relationship with him grew with her desire to raise Serenity in a "real" family with two parents. If she could give her daughter the security and love she herself had never felt as a child, she would do whatever it took to ensure Serenity lived a good life.

If Chassidy could do things differently, she would, but in real life there were no do-overs. Once she had made her decision to be married she tried her absolute best, despite her dissatisfaction, to be the best mother and wife she could be.

As Chassidy lay still in her bed on her 30th birthday, she thought about how much fun she could be having if she had agreed to hang out with her best friend, Kim, instead of rushing home after work in case Eric had finally decided to be romantic on this milestone birthday. Kim told her she would be waiting on invisible buses, but Chassidy hoped Kim was wrong. Now, looking around, she felt stupid. This was typical Eric.

The room was quiet, except for the sound of Chassidy breathing. She glanced at the clock on her nightstand. It was already midnight and Eric still hadn't made it home, nor had he called her at any time during the day to check in or wish her a happy birthday. She wondered where he was since he had been off work for at least six hours, but in her heart, she already knew. He hadn't cared to be discreet about his many indiscretions. She had hoped, however, that he would respect her enough as his wife and the mother of his child, to at least show up on her birthday.

Chassidy closed her eyes and tried to calm her racing mind. Oh how she despised Eric.

There was no way God desired her to be in the unhappy and loveless relationship she was in. To leave it all would mean being vulnerable to the unknown. To stay would mean to die a miserable woman and possibly raise a miserable child with misguided ideas about love and marriage.

All she knew was that she needed fresh air.

A final tear fell from her cheek and wet her silk pillow, leaving a circle beneath her eye.

God, please help me. Please! All I want is a man who will love me like You love me. I'm so tired of being unhappy. This hurts so bad! If my marriage is over, Lord, You end it. Please give me a sign that I can't ignore. Please, Lord. I promise I'll listen this time.

An hour later Chassidy heard the garage door open and shortly after that Eric flicked on the light, not seeming to care that his wife might be asleep.

"Where have you been?" Chassidy asked knowingly.

Eric wasn't much of a drinker, but he had obviously had one too many.

Eric headed to their en suite bathroom to relieve himself. When he finished, he flushed the toilet, washed his hands and plopped on the bed.

"The fellas and I had a few drinks after work."

"You didn't think to call and let me know?"

"Didn't think I'd be out this late. Misplaced my phone. Had to take a quick nap before I drove back," he rambled off before he dropped off to sleep.

"Did you even remember that today is my birthday?"

Eric responded with a snore.

This must be the sign.

A sense of peace washed over Chassidy.

Thank you, Lord.

She got up and looked at herself in the mirror that hung across from their bed. It was time for a change. Tonight would be the last night Eric would ever hurt her. Ever. She'd make sure of it. If he could go out and do his thing, so could she.

She turned off the light and laid back down as she mapped out her plan to get her groove back.

Starting tomorrow, it would be all about her.

1

Freak Him Girl Dress
✳ ✳ ✳

"Haaaaaay," Kim exclaimed as Chassidy hurriedly closed the passenger's side door of Kim's BMW X5. "Girl, look at you in your "freak him girl" dress! You trying to hurt some feelings tonight, ain't you?"

"This old thing?" Chassidy asked playfully as she rubbed her hands across her low-cut short black number. "But it's these heels that really set the outfit off," Chassidy said as she extended her leg onto Kim's steering wheel.

"Heffa, please put your leg down before someone gets the wrong idea," Kim laughed and shoved Chassidy's leg away.

"You know you want my body," Chassidy teased.

She made a kissy face and shimmied.

"You're a fool, Chassidy!" Kim laughed as she pulled away from the curb and sped toward the 91 freeway.

Chassidy exhaled loudly, "Girl! I am so happy to be out of that house. You have no idea."

Kim glanced at her. "I can only imagine."

"Let me tell you what this negro did today."

"Wait. You're not about to ruin our night out by complaining about your trifling soon-to-be ex-husband, are you? Because tonight is all about turning up. We can talk on the phone about him," Kim said matter-of-factly. "Whatever he did, you are out the house now, you got your 'freak him girl" dress on, you look good, and you're gonna pull some fine negroes tonight. I claim that in the mighty name of Jesus."

"You going to hell for that one, Kim," Chassidy laughed.

"Why I got to go to hell, heffa?" Kim laughed.

"Don't be involving Jesus in what I plan to do tonight. That's all I'm saying."

"Chassidy, you crazy. That's why you my girl! I've missed hanging out with your silly self."

"Hell, I missed hanging out with my silly self, too. But old Miss Sophia back now," Chassidy said as she channeled her inner Oprah from The Color Purple.

"Well it's about dang time, Miss Sophia. I've been having to handle these fine men out here in these Cali streets all by myself," Kim said as she took a sip of Red Bull.

She motioned for Chassidy to drink the unopened one in the cup holder.

"I'm sure you'd like that."

"I can't lie. The men love Kim and Kim loves them right back, but I have missed hanging out with you. Sheree and Andrea are too goody two shoes for me. I swear, I can't get my freak on 'cause they always need a ride back home and they're too bourgeois to catch an Uber."

"Well you don't have to worry about that with me. I definitely won't need a ride tonight."

"I heard that, Miss Thang," Kim said as she gave Chassidy a high five.

Chassidy took a sip of her energy drink and looked out the passenger's window.

Way too fast were the only words to describe Kim's driving. She really should have been giving Danica Patrick or Kyle Larson a run for their money on NASCAR tracks instead of endangering the lives of innocent people on the streets of L.A. Kim had been given so many tickets Chassidy couldn't quite understand how she still even had a license.

Chassidy made a note to either pick Kim up or meet her at the club next time.

Chassidy noticed a billboard of a couple gazing longingly into each other's eyes as the man refilled the woman's glass of Stella Rosa. It had been too long since anyone had looked at Chassidy that way. She sighed.

Kim glanced at her. "What's wrong?"

"Nothing. Just ready, that's all."

"I can drive a little faster, but I don't like to go over 100."

"Please don't drive any faster," Chassidy begged with a nervous laugh. "That's not at all what I meant. I'm just ready for change. I'm ready for better. I can't believe God put me on this earth to be as miserable as I've been for the past three years."

"He didn't. Misery is a choice you made, but tonight you are choosing to take the mechanical bull by the horn and ride it 'til they shut the place down."

"None of this is ever what I envisioned for my life, you know?" Chassidy said.

"Not tonight, Chassidy. Save it for another night."

As soon as Kim said that DJ Mustard's "Want Her" came up on the playlist and Kim hollered out, "This is my song!"

She turned the music up so loud that Chassidy could no longer hear herself think.

Kim sang along at the top of her lungs, waved her hands back and forth, and continued down the road.

Chassidy couldn't help but crack a smile. Kim was just who she needed to be with tonight because Kim wasn't going to allow her to do anything to make the night less enjoyable. Chassidy respected that. She took a deep breath and allowed herself to feel the music.

She bobbed her head to the beat.

"All the rich ones want you," Kim pointed and rapped to Chassidy with excited eyes.

Kim was all the way lit and Chassidy loved it!

Tonight was going to be one for the books.

2

Love in this Club

✳ ✳ ✳

Chassidy looked around and took everything in. It had been too long since she had stepped foot in a club. Before she got married, she was at the hottest clubs in LA almost every single weekend, but something about her idea of marriage and the malarkey of the club just didn't seem to go hand in hand.

During her life as a single woman the club had been where she went primarily for the purpose of meeting men. Some people went to see one of their favorite artists perform, others for the drinks or camaraderie, but for Chassidy none of those things had been the main attraction for her.

If a club didn't promise all of that plus some fine brothas who could take her out in the weeks, months, and possibly years that followed, she would have just stayed home.

Her favorite clubs had been the ones that were too expensive for men who still lived at home with their mothers. Chassidy reasoned if they couldn't afford to live on their own, there wasn't much they could do for her.

She avoided scrubs like the plague.

Although she had only been on the club scene for about five years when things got serious with Eric, she hadn't grown tired of it at all. Because she had downplayed her love of the club to Eric, they never went together. He was a square, so he wasn't into the club and taking him would have been like taking sand to the beach, so she kept the two separate.

She and Kim continued to party while she dated Eric, but when she got pregnant with Skylar, everything changed. Chassidy had decided long ago that she would not be the pregnant lady at the club, so when she found herself with child, she figured it was God's way of confirming that it was indeed time to slow it down. And once she said "I do," she just stayed away altogether, mostly out of respect for the institution of marriage.

Looking around tonight it seemed that so much had changed. A bigger percentage of the chicks looked more like the Kardashians than they had five years ago. Chassidy figured that would work to her advantage. People get tired of monotony.

Everyone looked so much alike that Kim and Chassidy were definitely a breath of sexy fresh air. They were the baddest ladies in the club, without a doubt—natural God-given voluptuousness couldn't be beat.

The dance floor, although it was crowded, didn't seem as cramped as it had in Chassidy's heyday.

The DJ was playing "Get Low," an oldie considering, but Chassidy didn't have any complaints! That was one of her favorite songs! The crowd didn't seem to have any complaints, either.

They sang along and waved their hands from side to side. Chassidy laughed to herself as she thought about how she used to get on her hands and knees and groove to this jam back in the day.

None of these new ladies could get down with her if they tried. She could just look at them and tell they were too prissy or too inexperienced to know how to work their assets.

Kim was on the dance floor pressed up against a guy who was a little too short to get any real action from her, Chassidy thought, but they appeared to be having the time of their lives. Chassidy smiled at her friend. Kim was never the one to turn down a dance and she was extremely kind to suitors, regardless of whether they actually had a chance with her or not.

That was one of Chassidy's favorite reasons for partying with her—she was up for anything, down for whatever, and just downright fun.

Chassidy took a sip of her *Adios*, courtesy of a flirty man at the bar who was old enough to be her grandfather. She tried to deny the drink because she didn't want to get his senior citizen hopes up, but he insisted he just wanted to do something nice for her and didn't expect anything in return.

He was a man of his word, and the *Adios* was the best she had ever had. On the dance floor she two stepped seductively as she held the drink in her left hand and waved her right arm in unison with the rest of the crowd.

Her "freak him girl dress" had gotten her quite a bit of attention, but aside from bar grandpa and a few other ballsy brothas with absolutely no hope whatsoever of seeing her outside of the club *ever* again after that night, no one had made a serious move. There was one man in particular who had caught her eye a couple times, but she couldn't tell if the woman he was with was his girl or just his friend.

She didn't mind a little friendly competition, but she didn't need any more drama than what she already had going on at home. The point of the next man was to *physically* release... not to add additional stress. As she continued to dance, she detected that the cutie was checking her out.

He licked his succulent lips as his "friend" stood with her arm around his neck and whispered something in his ear. He nodded and then the woman glanced at Chassidy, blew a kiss, and waved.

Chassidy wasn't expecting that, so she glanced around to see if they were both looking at her.

They were.

Tonight was about going home with a fine man... not trying new things with a fine man and his woman, so she took a long sip of her drink and looked away from handsome and his "friend."

They were obviously hoping for something a little freakier than what Chassidy had in mind.

To the windows...to the walls.

Chassidy was really feeling herself, her drink, and the song. A few beats later, she felt the familiar pelvic thrust of someone looking to take advantage of a fine tipsy woman on the dance floor.

She was game.

Without looking back, she decided to give this guy a chance. It was obvious he was working with a nice package because she could feel its dimensions and excitement against her rear end.

From the way he moved, she could tell he knew how to handle the full figure that was Chassidy's.

His scent was right and his hands touched her body in all the right places to let her know she wasn't working with a rookie. No need to turn around and possibly ruin a good thing, so Chassidy relaxed into her partner and rocked with him.

He kept up well.

They danced to a few more fast songs before the DJ slowed things down and mixed in Usher's "Love in this Club." Chassidy and her partner grinded like long-time lovers whose bodies were perfectly in sync. He embraced her from the back.

His excitement hadn't subsided since they first connected. Chassidy 5'10" frame felt protected by the at least 6'6" man who held on to her.

God, she hoped he looked decent enough to justify the five songs she had spent dancing with him.

"I like the way you move," he said.

She couldn't imagine that voice belonging to a mud duck so she closed her eyes, smiled, and hoped this man was as fine as he sounded.

"What's your name?" he asked.

"Janae," Chassidy said. Her middle name was good enough for tonight.

"Janae? I like that," he said. "Where's your man, Janae?"

"He's not here tonight," Chassidy said.

He must have liked that answer because his mouth slowly made its way from her ear to her neck.

His soft full lips made themselves at home on her neck. Something about this man's presence relaxed her in an unexpected way. His tongue made figure eights on her neck and she imagined how it would feel if he did that exact same thing to a few other places on her body.

Chassidy closed her eyes and let out a soft moan.

"You're so sexy," he said and turned her to face him.

When Chassidy looked at her mystery man, she was taken aback. It was the fine man she had seen with his "friend" from earlier. She hadn't seen either of them in a while, but no part of her had imagined that he was the one she had been dancing with.

"What's wrong?" he asked.

"I didn't realize *you* were my dance partner," she said and smiled.

"Are you disappointed?"

"Depends. Are you with your girlfriend tonight?"

"I'm trying to be with you tonight," he responded.

"Is that right? Well, I'm not trying to wreck any happy homes."

"How about this? I'm single, but I really want to be taken by you."

Chassidy smiled. She liked the way he talked. He was confident and sexy, two things that made her want to give it to him right there on the dance floor. And the truth was, whatever his relationship was with his "friend," it couldn't be too serious considering he had danced so many songs with Chassidy. And if they were together, there was no way he should be so comfortable kissing her the way he had with his girl somewhere nearby.

Chassidy decided she would just have fun and see what happened. That was the point of tonight anyway.

"So what's your name?" Chassidy asked.

"Donovan," he replied.

"Well, it's nice to meet you Donovan," Chassidy said.

"Let me buy you another drink," he said gesturing toward her empty cup.

Chassidy nodded her head and with her hand in his allowed him to direct her to the bar.

On the way over she noticed that Kim was still on the dance floor. The DJ had started the reggae mix, Kim's specialty, and she was letting her Jamaican roots come all the way out. Chassidy smiled at her.

When Kim saw her and the man, whose hand she held, Kim gave her two thumbs up and mouthed, "Yaaaaas, boo. Yaaaaaas."

Chassidy laughed and raised her glass.

Sherry Berry

3

The Answer to Life's Problems

∗ ∗ ∗

The valet pulled up in Kim's BMW and ran to the passenger's side to let Chassidy in and then back to the driver's side to help Kim in and collect his tip.

"I'm sorry for messing up your action, girl," Chassidy apologized once they pulled off.

"Don't worry about it. I wasn't feeling anybody tonight anyway."

"Really? The way you were grooving with that Ginuwine looking brotha, I just knew he was gonna get some action."

"Girl, no. I was feeling him before he opened his mouth. His breath smelled like straight sewage. I offered him gum and breath mints a few times, but he didn't get the point. It's a daggone shame to look that good and have breath that bad."

Chassidy couldn't hold back her laughter. "You are still the same...an absolute mess."

"I'm telling the truth, Chassidy. His breath was offensive. He all but gave me a case of the bubble guts with his rotten self."

Chassidy laughed so hard tears streamed down her face.

"Rotten? Dang, Kim! You a cold piece."

"Rotten," Kim confirmed and joined in the laughter.

"So what did your dude say about ol' girl he was with?"

"He told me not to worry about her. He's single. But something about the way she kept looking at us made me uncomfortable."

"Girl! The way he was all up on you there's no way they're *together* together."

"I don't know."

"I'm just saying. If that was my man, I would go straight Lorena Bobbitt on his behind. I refuse to be disrespected. Especially not in public."

"I'm with you, but nowadays, you never know. People are down with all kinds of kinky stuff. Not this chick right here though. What I've got is so good that a brotha doesn't need anything extra," Chassidy said as she pointed to her unmentionables and bounced to the music that played in the background.

"I know that's right, girl," Kim said and laughed.

"I'mma keep it real though. I *did* slip him my number."

"What?"

"Kim, that man was fine and I'm in heat."

"He *was* fine," Kim agreed.

"We'll see if he hits me up."

"He will," Kim said. "Trust me."

"If he can pull himself away from ol' girl."

"He'll make time. They always do," Kim said.

Chassidy looked out the window at yet another Stella Rosa billboard. Whoever came up with the idea of placing them strategically along both the north and south sides of the 405 freeway was brilliant. Whether coming or going, sitting in traffic or cruising at 70 miles per hour, those ads made Chassidy feel like the answer to life's problems was a nice sweet intoxicating drink and the company of an attractive attentive man. She sighed.

"Oh shoot," Kim hollered out as "Action" came on the playlist. She turned up the music and sang.

Chassidy joined in and they drowned out Terror Fabulous as Kim sped down the freeway.

Just before they pulled up at Chassidy's house, Kim adjusted the music to a respectful level.

"Are you gonna be alright? You know you are always welcome at my place."

"Thank you. I'll be alright.

"What do you have planned for tomorrow? Do you want to try to get up again?"

"I for sure have to do laundry tomorrow. It's been a few weeks since I've washed and if I don't get to it tomorrow I'll have to go to work commando on Monday."

"Ain't nothing wrong with letting your cookie breathe," Kim said as she pursed her lips and exhaled slowly.

"Girl, stop! You are crazy," Chassidy laughed. "Seriously though, I might be able to get up tomorrow night after Serenity goes to bed, but I'll let you know."

"Ok, hit me up. I'm trying to take advantage of this time before you decide to try to work things out with Eric."

"That isn't happening. I'm done. For real," Chassidy said firmly, more to herself than Kim.

"Alright then, Miss Lady. Well, I *might* see you tomorrow night, chica."

Chassidy smiled and opened the door.

"Good night," she paused. "And thank you. I needed this."

"What you need is something that starts with a d and ends with a k, but I ain't the one to gossip," Kim whispered.

Chassidy laughed and shook her head. "Good night," she said again. Standing in front of the door, Chassidy paused and took a deep breath before returning to the reality of Eric.

4

The Right One
✳ ✳ ✳

Chassidy sat in the plush office chair the branch receptionist, Sam, had recently ordered for her. The chair was perfect. It had become one of the highlights of Chassidy's demanding job as an account manager for one of the largest banks in Los Angeles. On Wednesday afternoons, if foot traffic was low, Chassidy made calls to her clients to make sure they were happy with their investments and to see if they had any concerns. This was one of the slow days and Chassidy welcomed it.

She took a short break to check out a new clothing website Sam had mentioned to her. So far, Chassidy loved the concept. You paid a small monthly fee and based on a style survey taken during registration, the company would send you a box of new clothes every other week. If ever you received something you didn't like or something that didn't fit, you simply mailed it back to the company and they would send a replacement outfit better suited to your taste. Whoever thought of the idea was genius. Chassidy had already decided it was time to revamp her mingling attire and there was a "Night on the Town" section that would have her looking fly in no time, and it could be done without the stressors that came along with the normal retail experience.

Last weekend came and went without too much more excitement. Laundry took up more time than Chassidy anticipated, so her recap with Kim was postponed until the upcoming weekend. Chassidy had already secured a babysitter in case Eric refused to watch Serenity. Their communication had never been great, but ever since the birthday debacle, things had been increasingly strained.

When they first started dating, they would call and text each other all day long. There was no doubt in Chassidy's mind that she was a priority to Eric because he didn't make a move without asking her thoughts about it first. He wasn't great when it came to romancing her, so Chassidy knew not to expect flowers or foot massages or to hear "I love you's" from him. She couldn't deny that his attention in the beginning stages said what his words did not. Soon after they married, his actions and his words no longer gave any hint of affection. It became more difficult to give him the benefit of the doubt and Chassidy realized that he didn't act or speak in a loving way because he didn't love her. He had never loved her. That truth was confirmed a few months back.

"Look, I'm just saying you need to be a little more considerate. Next time, just call me or text me before you decide to hang out after work. That's the least you could do."

"Chassidy, I'm a grown man. I don't have to get your permission to do anything."

"Eric, no part of what I'm saying is about you asking my permission to do anything. I get that you

wanted to relax with your friends and I'm fine with that. Lord knows I could stand to hang out a little myself. What I'm talking about is called being considerate. I thought you were coming straight home after work. I made dinner for you. I told Serenity you would be home to eat with us and play with her. I called and texted you more times than I'd ever advise a woman to reach out to a man who hasn't responded to her. Why? Because you didn't tell me that you weren't coming straight home after work. I was worried, Eric. Out of respect for me, you should have called," she finished as tears streamed down her face at her heart-felt speech.

Eric looked at her and offered no sense of remorse. Then he said what Chassidy had sensed long ago.

"You know, I'm still trying to figure out why I ever married you," Eric said.

Chassidy gasped. She wasn't expecting that response. Where did that even come from?

Eric continued, "I didn't call because I didn't think to call you. I didn't come straight here after work because I didn't want to see your face. I'm here right now because this is where my boys told the

Uber to drop me off. I'd much rather be anywhere else and I swear if it wasn't for Serenity, I never would have married you."

Chassidy looked at Eric and her heart broke as it had so many times during their relationship. This time she knew that all the crazy glue in the world couldn't put it back together again. Even though Eric was almost always cold, none of what he had ever said hurt as badly as his confession that night. She could smell the alcohol on his breath and knew that his liquid courage was the result of it. What he said was his truth.

It hurt to hear him say it, but it hurt even more to think about all that she, herself, had sacrificed to be with him. It hurt because Chassidy knew exactly what he meant. She understood what it was like to feel trapped with someone you didn't love because she lived that truth every day. She could say with certainty that if it weren't for Serenity, she never would have married Eric. She couldn't count the number of times she asked herself why she ever agreed to go out with him or why she continued to go out with him. Why she was intimate with him or why she was intimate with him again and again, even though he never satisfied her? Why she didn't protect herself while she was intimate with a man who she didn't really like all that much or why she agreed to marry him when he found out she was pregnant. Why? She absolutely understood what Eric felt, but she cared enough about him not to ever say any of that to him.

That conversation was on a loop for Chassidy. She thought about it every single day and every day she got the same sinking feeling.

Chassidy's cellphone buzzed and snapped her back to reality. It was a number she didn't recognize.

"This is Chassidy."

There was no response. Chassidy looked at the phone to make sure the person was still on the line.

"Hello?"

"Uh. Yes. I'm calling to speak with Janae."

Chassidy's heart raced. She had only given that name to one person and the bass voice on the other end matched the one of the fine man she knew it belonged to.

"Why hello, handsome."

"Is this Janae?"

"First name Chassidy, middle name Janae."

"Oh, I see," Donovan said with a slight laugh. "So which do you normally go by?"

"Which do *you* prefer?"

Donovan paused for a moment. "I like Chassidy. It fits you."

"Oh really?"

"I know I haven't been able to stop thinking about you. You already got me tipsy and I haven't even had a taste."

"Ok. I see you've got game," Chassidy teased.

"Not at all. I'm sure with a name like Chassidy and moves like you've got guys get drunk off you all the time."

"Perhaps," Chassidy said coyly. "But it only matters if the right one takes a sip, right?"

Donovan laughed. "I like that."

"Do you?"

"I do. I want to take more than a sip."

Chassidy wanted him to take more than a sip, too.

"Is that right?"

"Absolutely. That's why I'm calling. I'd love to take you out Saturday."

"This Saturday?"

"Well, unless you're busy."

Chassidy shifted. Going out with him *this* Saturday meant she would have to schedule time for nails and hair. She would also have to make a trip to the mall because *nothing* in her closet would work and her wardrobe subscription wouldn't start until the following week. Plus, she already had plans with Kim. Of course, those plans could be rescheduled, but she couldn't let Donovan know he had it like that just yet.

"I feel like I have something to do Saturday, but I don't have my calendar in front of me," Chassidy said. "What time are you thinking and where would we be going?"

"Six o' clock P.M. Chace Park in Marina del Rey."

"The park?"

"Yeah. They have this concert series there all this month. Billy Ocean is performing Saturday. I figure we can do the whole beach picnic thing and then go grab a bite at The Yard House."

Chassidy smiled. "Sweet. Ok, I'll text you later on today to let you know one way or the other."

"Alright. I sure hope you can make it happen."

Chassidy smiled.

"Look, one of my clients just walked in. I'm going to have to give you a call back," Donovan said.

"No problem at all. Have a good day."

"You too, Chassidy Janae. Oh, and I'm *the right one* you mentioned earlier."

"Is that right?" she asked. "You'll have to show me."

"I'm looking forward to it," he said.

5

Not-so Slight Change of Plans

✻ ✻ ✻

It was Chassidy's day to pick up Serenity from daycare, so she left work a little early to give herself time to shop for her date with Donovan. One of the perks of being in management was that she could work a flexible schedule. She didn't take advantage of that perk often, but today was slow so she figured it couldn't hurt.

There were a few boutique options Chassidy preferred over malls and none of them were near where she lived. She would have to make the best of her time and be on the road by five P.M. to get to

Serenity before late fees were tacked on to the already exorbitant prices the center charged. Chassidy decided to take a chance at the boutiques near her job in Culver City because they carried unique pieces. She went for those boutiques because she wouldn't have to worry about seeing anyone else from her circle wearing any of the same outfits. The items were pricey, but the salespeople were eager to help and Chassidy welcomed all the help she could get.

"Oh, that looks good on you," Jane, the sales associate complimented enthusiastically.

Jane looked like she had just stepped off of the cover of Vogue's latest issue.

Whenever a sales associate as fabulous as herself complimented Chassidy on her fabulousness after she had chosen an item, they could consider it purchased. Chassidy knew she was gullible this way, but she couldn't help it. In her mind, being recognized as fly by someone else who was even more put together than she was was the pinnacle of what it meant to "slay."

"Are you sure? You've said that about all the outfits I've tried on."

"You know why? Because you're gorgeous and look amazing in whatever you put on."

Chassidy looked herself over in the full length mirror that hung in her fitting room.

Pleased with what she saw, she smiled. "I wouldn't say all that."

"No, seriously."

The outfit did hug her body in all the right places. She couldn't deny that she looked good. "Well, thank you."

"Just calling it like I see it," Jane said, "But if I had to choose, this one is my favorite. And it's on sale, so you can't go wrong."

"Please tell me you have the perfect shoes to wear with this," Chassidy said, hoping to kill a couple birds with one stone.

"You said you're going to the park and then dinner, right?"

"Right."

"So you're gonna need something comfortable but sexy. I do have the perfect shoe," Jane said as she sauntered over to a pair of turquoise pumps. "What size do you wear?"

"I'm a 9," Chassidy said.

The associate brought back a pair of shoes. They were simple, but cute—perfect for Chassidy's date with Donovan. "Our shoes run a little big, so I brought you an 8 ½. Let me know what you think."

"I don't need to try them on. I trust you. What's your return policy?"

"Exchange only. Products must be unworn," Jane as if she were quoting from her training manual.

"Perfect. If I have any problems with the shoes, I'll just exchange them tomorrow on my lunch break."

"Alright. I'll start ringing you up."

"Thanks, Jane."

Chassidy glanced at her cell phone and noticed that she had two missed calls from Eric. *Strange.* He never called at this time of day. She hoped everything was alright. After paying for her items, thanking God for such an unusually pleasant experience, and bidding Jane farewell, Chassidy made her way to the car and called Eric.

"Is everything alright?" Chassidy asked as soon as he picked up the phone.

"Everything is fine. I called the office but Sam said you had already left for the day."

"Oh, yeah. I had a coffee meeting with a client," Chassidy lied. She was surprised by how easily it slipped off her tongue. "It's already 5:10, so I'm praying that I'm not late to the daycare." Chassidy shifted the car into drive and made her way toward Venice Boulevard and the 10 freeway.

"Well look, I've been thinking," he said. "Things have been pretty crazy between us lately. I know I'm to blame for a lot of it. I'm not the best at this sort of thing, but I want to make everything up to you."

Where is this coming from?

Chassidy removed the phone from her ear and looked at the screen to be sure it was Eric she was talking to.

"So I booked us a trip to Catalina. We leave Friday and get back Sunday."

Chassidy was silent. She couldn't believe her ears. A few months ago hearing Eric say these words would have meant the world to her, but today all she could think about was how she would have to cancel her date with Donovan. She had just spent $320 on shoes and an outfit that she couldn't return. Alone on an island with Eric? They barely had a single pleasant conversation in months. What would it be like to be alone with him?

"That's sweet of you, Eric, but you know I have to work on Friday. And where would Serenity be?"

"I've already handled all that. I told Sam that you won't be able to make it Friday and my mom is going to keep Serenity."

"Really?" Chassidy asked as she searched for another excuse.

She couldn't think of anything that outweighed her husband desiring to take her away to Catalina. She had tried to get him to take her there on multiple occasions, but he said he had no desire to go on a cruise, even if it was just a short one. For him to plan this trip showed that he was willing to put his feelings to the side to do something that would make her happy. That was a step in the right direction. Maybe this would be just what they needed to spark the romance their relationship lacked. She felt guilty for even considering not going.

And even though Donovan was fine with moves better than Jagger's, she'd rather take a chance on her marriage than have any doubts about what could have been with Eric if she had just been a better wife.

"You don't seem excited," Eric said.

She could hear a twinge of disappointment in his voice.

"I'm sorry, babe. You really just caught me off guard. I wasn't expecting any of this. But this is so sweet of you, Eric. I'd very much like to go with you to Catalina. Thank you."

"Oh, and I know how you are about your hair and outfits, so I made you an appointment with Alexis and I bought you a couple things to wear. I hope you like them."

What? Who is this man on the phone?

"Really? You thought of everything, didn't you? Thanks, babe!"

"I'm trying, Chas'."

"I see that. And I appreciate it. What time will you be home tonight? I've had a long day so I'm just gonna pick up pizza."

"I should be there by 7. Can you get me a salad, too?"

"Of course. See you soon."

"Thanks. Alright. Later."

When Eric hung up the phone, Chassidy took a deep breath. That call from Eric was nothing short of a miracle. She had no idea what had come over him, but she welcomed it. God could do anything. He could breathe life into dead things, right? Eric's call was an example of that.

The next three things on Chassidy's agenda were to call Kim and tell her the unbelievable turn of events, pick up Serenity, and text Donovan to let him know that she wouldn't be able to make it Saturday.

6

The Answer to a Prayer
✳ ✳ ✳

Eric looked dapper in his all-white linen button down and shorts. His shirt was open just enough to reveal his well-sculpted dark chocolate chest. His shorts hugged his toned body in all the right places and his mahogany sandals looked like they cost a small fortune. Eric's sense of style was on pointe. He looked polished in whatever he wore.

Today, Eric's 6'5" stature, crisp threads, fresh haircut, dark shades, and Louis Vuitton carry-on commanded the attention of the other passengers on the Catalina Express. Chassidy could see their wheels turning as they tried to figure out whether Eric was an actor or professional athlete. She knew he was eating it all up. She smiled adoringly at him. He grabbed her hand and flashed his pearly whites.

"Thank you for being here. I know it was last minute, but I feel really bad about missing your birthday. I'm going to make it up to you, Chas. I'm going to be a better husband."

Chassidy couldn't see his eyes but she could hear the sincerity in his voice.

"I really appreciate this, Eric. Thank you."

Chassidy closed her eyes and basked in the wind as it whipped across her face. She couldn't believe this was happening. She couldn't believe that she was in this moment with her husband. This was all she wanted. Their relationship had been so strained that she hadn't imagined Eric putting together something so romantic on his own.

This entire trip and the planning that went into it was out of character for him, but Chassidy liked it.

Maybe this was the answer to her prayer. She had heard that God gave beauty for ashes. Maybe things would only get better for them. Maybe this was the start of her fairytale life with Eric.

Chassidy sighed and opened her eyes. The water, the sky, the weather, her husband— in this moment, everything was perfect.

Chassidy hadn't felt any attraction to Eric in a long time. So much had happened. But today was different. She hoped today would be the start of something beautiful. Chassidy welcomed those long forgotten emotions and sensations and looked forward to showing Eric just how much this meant to her. She was going to do that as soon as they made it to their hotel room. The hotel room couldn't come quickly enough. She needed to release.

Once the Catalina Express docked, Chassidy and Eric made their way, hand in hand onto the boardwalk, where a concierge stood near a golf cart and held a sign that read "Good." Chassidy glanced at Eric, who walked confidently over to him.

"I'm Eric Good," he said, extending his hand toward the concierge.

"Mr. Good, nice to meet you. My name is Jeff and I will be your personal guide while you are here in Catalina."

Chassidy couldn't believe this. Their own personal guide? Eric had really gone all out this time.

"And this beauty must be," Jeff began, as he reached for Chassidy's hand.

"This is my wife, Chassidy," Eric interrupted.

Jeff's brow furrowed as he shook Chassidy's hand. He looked at Eric and then back at Chassidy.

"Chassidy? What a lovely name."

"Thank you," she blushed.

"Have you two ever been here before?" Jeff asked as he took their bags from them and placed them on the passenger's side of the cart.

"No. Chassidy's been wanting to come here for a while though. This is a belated birthday getaway."

"I see," Jeff said, "Well, welcome to Catalina. I'm sure you'll love this little island as much as I do." He paused for a moment as he seemed to search for the right words.

"I'm sure we will. This place looks so amazing. It's like a whole other world and we're only an hour away from home. I'm not sure why it has taken me so long to make this trip," Chassidy said.

"If you feel that way now, just wait until you take the tour. You won't want to leave," Jeff said and then paused before continuing, "Well, my intentions were to take you two to the hotel first so you could relax and get changed before you hit the beach, but I actually think it would be best to lounge a little first. I still have some last minute changes I need to make to your room."

Jeff looked at Eric as if he was trying to send subliminal messages.

Eric kept his eyes on Chassidy. "Are you hungry? Because if so, Original Jack's Country Kitchen is the place to go. They serve really good breakfast."

"What do you want to do, Chas?" Eric asked.

Chassidy couldn't believe it. Eric had never asked her what she wanted to do. He always just made plans for them that only considered what he wanted. This was nice. Chassidy was ready to hit the sheets and show her appreciation to her man, but the day was still early and breakfast wasn't such a bad idea.

"Original Jack's sounds good to me," Chassidy said.

"I assure you the room will be ready for you by the time you finish," Jeff said.

"Well alright. Original Jack's it is," Eric said.

"To get there you're just going to head that way," Jeff pointed down a row of restaurants and shops. "In about a minute, you'll see it on your right hand side. I'm going to take the bags to your room but I'll be sitting right here once you finish eating. Meet me then and we'll talk about your plan for the day."

"Alright, my man," Eric said, "Thanks. We'll see you soon."

"Take your time," Jeff encouraged.

Eric nodded his head and they headed, hand in hand, for the restaurant.

Chassidy was so impressed by it all. She still couldn't believe that Eric had been thoughtful enough to plan things out so well. They had been on a few trips together over the years and never had they had a personal concierge or tour guide. Jeff's services must have cost a small fortune. Chassidy liked to think she was worth it to Eric. She hoped breakfast was quick because she couldn't stop thinking about all that she wanted to do to show her husband her appreciation.

"You're mighty quiet," Eric said. "What's on your mind?"

"I'm sorry, babe. I'm just so happy. I don't know what to say."

Eric smiled and kissed Chassidy on her forehead.

"This is only the beginning," Eric said. "Wait until you see the view from the helicopter."

"Helicopter?" Chassidy let out an excited squeal. "Oh my God. Eric, you really did well."

"I know it seems like I don't listen, but I do. I knew you would have a good time here with me."

Chassidy smiled. She put her arm around Eric's waist and rested her head on his chiseled shoulder as they strolled toward the restaurant. This felt good.

The aroma of hot syrup and Applewood bacon filled the air and reminded Chassidy that she normally ate breakfast before 6 in the morning. She hoped Original Jack's was as good as Jeff said because she was feeling a little hungry.

As they walked into the restaurant Chassidy was surprised to see so many patrons already seated. There wasn't a line outside and the place looked a lot larger on the inside than it did from the outside.

"Welcome to Original Jack's. How many are in your party?"

"40 if you count my imaginary crew. If not, it's just my wife and me," Eric said with a hearty laugh.

The hostess seemed unimpressed but she gave him a courtesy laugh and picked up a couple of menus. "Right this way," she said as she escorted them to a cozy booth near the kitchen. "Your server will be right with you," she said and walked back to her post near the front door.

"Babe, why do you always do that? You know your jokes are not funny."

"What do you mean, not funny? I was almost voted class clown in middle school."

"Well...everything is funny when you're in middle school, but um, that ship sailed years ago," Chassidy teased.

"Whatever."

"Good morning. My name is Renee and I'll be your server today. Would you like to hear our specials?"

"No," Eric replied, "but I would like to order two mimosas to get us started."

"Coming right up," Renee said as she made her way to the kitchen.

"You know, it may sound crazy but you seem so comfortable here. From the boat ride to spotting Jeff, to making all these arrangements. Are you sure you've never been here before?"

Eric shifted in his seat a little and cleared his throat. "Chas, you know how I am about research. I've been planning this trip for a while but now seemed like the perfect time to do it. Don't you agree?"

"I do. Thank you again, Eric," Chassidy said. "You have no idea how much this means to me. A week ago this time I was feeling like there wasn't any hope for us, but now I believe we could learn to love each other again."

"Yeah. It's gonna take some work to get things right but I'm willing to do whatever it takes. You've been good to me. Sorry I've been such a jerk."

Chassidy was taken aback. She had never heard Eric apologize to anyone for anything. He had even found a way to shift the blame from himself the time the two of them got into a heated argument that turned into a fight shortly after they were married.

The fight concluded with Chassidy's sliced finger, blood everywhere, and a trip to the emergency room.

Chassidy still hated to think about how upset they'd been that day... or how lucky Eric was lucky to still be alive. Chassidy had a few male cousins who would have done some serious damage to Eric if they ever heard the truth about what happened. Instead, Chassidy told everyone that she accidentally sliced her finger while chopping cabbage.

There was no denying how stupid she felt for staying with a man who had done such a horrible thing to her and made no apology for it, but she was a hopeless romantic. She wanted a family more than anything and she believed him when he said it would never happen again.

They had heated disagreements after that, but one of them would leave before either of them got mad enough to physically hurt each other.

She took his current apology to cover everything that he had put her through. She had never been one to hold a grudge, even though the average person would agree that she had every reason to.

"We both could have done a lot of things differently. I forgive you."

"Two mimosas," the waitress interrupted as she set the drinks down on the table. "We make the best mimosas on the island, so I've been told."

"According to Yelp, quite a few people agree with you," Eric said as he took a sip. "This is good."

Renee smiled. "Are you ready to order?"

"Please give us a few more minutes," Eric said as he picked up the menu for the first time since sitting.

"Alrighty. I'll be back to check on you soon."

Chassidy smiled admiringly at Eric while she watched him take the lead on their date. This was something she had wanted for a long time.

She thought back to the night of her birthday when she asked God to give her a man who would love her like He did. She sighed. Perhaps Eric had been growing into that man all along.

7

Breathless

✳ ✳ ✳

Chassidy gasped. "Oh my God, babe. This is beautiful," she said as she took in the palatial suite that Eric had reserved for them.

Eric looked pleased. "I'm glad you like it."

"I love it," Chassidy said, taking it all in. She walked into the kitchen and picked up a bottle of wine from the marble counter. Attached was a note. Chassidy read it aloud, "I can't stop thinking about you, today...tomorrow...always." She smiled at Eric as he walked across the living room and pulled back the drapes.

"Babe, this bottle of wine left such a beautiful note for me." She hugged the bottle and gave it a kiss.

"I feel the same way about you, Risata," she said to the royal blue bottle.

Eric looked at her and shook his head.

"Girl, you are crazy."

Chassidy set the bottle down and smiled. "All I know is that you'd better up your game. This bottle of wine is trying to take your spot."

"Is that right?" Eric asked as he softly kissed Chassidy on the neck.

She felt her legs buckle beneath her like never before and Eric wrapped his arms around her waist to steady her.

"Can that bottle of wine make you feel like that?" Eric teased.

Chassidy could feel her heart racing. She smiled naughtily at her husband. "I'm not sure what's come over you, Mr. Good, but I like it."

Eric pulled her into another embrace and pressed his plump lips against hers. Chassidy wanted this moment to last forever.

I want to show you something," Eric said as he pulled away. He took her hand into his.

Chassidy stood with her eyes closed for a moment until Eric gave a slight tug to snap her out of her bliss.

"Follow me." Eric led her down a short hallway and opened massive white double doors that led into an enormous bedroom. It was the size of their kitchen and living room put together at home.

On the bed, red rose petals were delicately laid into the shape of a heart. Chocolate covered strawberries were on a silver platter in the middle.

Eric headed to the dresser and flipped on the surround sound stereo. R. Kelly's "Feeling on Your Booty," pulsed through the speakers. This was Chassidy's song. Anything R. Kelly immediately turned her all the way on.

The drapes were pulled back, revealing what had to be the most beautiful view from the entire hotel. Chassidy walked toward the sliding glass doors that led to a balcony that wrapped around the suite. She hadn't noticed it until now, but this place really was like a picture pulled right from her vision board. She walked outside and took a deep breath.

"Eric, this is..."

Eric smiled as he joined her, "I knew you would like it." He gave her a soft kiss on the neck.

"I love it! I could sit out here all day. It's so beautiful."

"Wait until you see the sunset."

Chassidy looked at him and raised an eyebrow. "How do you..."

"Yelp. I read about the view on Yelp," he interrupted.

"Ok, ok," Chassidy smiled. "I'll have to remember to write the founder of Yelp a thank you letter for helping my husband get everything so right."

"Well, be prepared to write a whole lot of letters. This is only the beginning."

Chassidy looked around and took it all in. From where she stood she could see tourists lounging on white reclining beach chairs at Descanso Beach as the waves crashed on the shore. Swimmers and waders were sprinkled throughout the water and she could see a group of bikini clad ladies wearing big hats and neon colored sheer bikini coverings taking selfies.

Chassidy took a deep breath and sighed. Adina Howard's "T-shirt and Panties," pumped through the speakers. The last song was her song, but *this* was her *song*.

She turned to face Eric, but he was no longer by her side. She walked back into the bedroom and could hear water running in the bathroom.

Chassidy smiled.

Eric was predictable in most ways—a creature of habit. They had never made love without taking a shower first. That wasn't always convenient and had been one of the reasons they didn't make love as often as most newlyweds seemed to make in the early years of their own marriage. The showers had to be taken *right* before the intimacy and after long days at work or spending time with Serenity Chassidy often preferred sleep over the hassle of following all the rules that made Eric comfortable.

Chassidy would have loved to get it on like animals every once in a while—to be so passionately into one another that there wasn't time for a shower beforehand. But with Eric, there was never foreplay, with the exception of kisses on the neck. Oral wasn't an option for him. He told her about a bad experience one of his friends had in college—one that left his friend with embarrassing outbreaks and Eric scarred by the thought of putting his mouth anywhere near south of the border. As a result, Eric and Chassidy stuck to basic love-making.

They would start off in missionary and then transition to doggy—every time.

Chassidy knew that shortly after the shift to the second position things would be over soon. It was completely different than what she had experienced with other partners, but then again, none of them had ever offered to make her a wife. Mundane sex was a small price to pay for that title.

Chassidy thought it would be nice to join Eric in the shower. After all, they hadn't showered together since the early days. Maybe Eric would get caught up in the mood and make love to her in the shower, but even if that didn't go down it would be nice to have him scrub her back.

Chassidy removed her clothes and glanced in the large mirror that hung above the cherrywood dresser. She looked good. Her body was as tight as it had been in college. There was no evidence that her tummy had ever housed another human being.

She blew herself a kiss and walked toward the bathroom door when Eric's phone, which sat comfortably on the nightstand, began vibrating like crazy. Chassidy's first thought was to ignore it, but then she realized it might be Eric's mom calling to say there was a problem with Serenity.

She walked to the nightstand and picked it up. A series of text messages from Ayesha popped up.

There was no way this could be the same Ayesha he had cheated with over a year ago. Eric promised that things were over between the two of them.

Chassidy slid her finger across the phone and saw that they had been texting each other naughty messages and pictures for at least a month. They texted about all sorts of rendezvous, plans for Eric to leave Chassidy, how much they missed each other, and all the things they wanted to do to each other.

There were so many texts.

Chassidy looked through his call log and realized that Eric and Angela spent a great deal of time talking. The hours of the calls were troublesome as well. Quite a few of them were during hours when Chassidy thought Eric was sound asleep next to her. In actuality, he must have been sneaking to another room to talk with his mistress.

Chassidy went back into his messages and scrolled through them a little more slowly this time. Her eyes filled with tears. All of this had been a lie.

Should she confront Eric or get dressed and walk out with some of her dignity?

Oh God, why?

Just then Chassidy saw a message from Ayesha that read, *Hey sexy. I won't be able to make it to Catalina after all.* Chassidy gasped and continued reading, *My stepfather took a turn for the worst. Moms is pretty upset. She needs me to be with her this weekend. I'll make it up to you.* That message ended with the sad face and kissy face emojis.

Eric had responded with *Don't worry about it. We can go some other time. You need to be there for your mom.*

Ayesha responded, *That's why I love you.*

I love you too, Chassidy read and threw the phone across the room.

She couldn't remember the last time Eric had said or written those words to her. Her heart ached.

She quickly dressed and gathered her things. She couldn't breathe. She needed air.

Eric hurried into the room with a towel wrapped around his waist.

"Chassidy, are you alright?"

Chassidy looked at him with tears streaming down her face.

"You lied to me...and I'm done," she said as she exited the bedroom and walked toward the front door.

"Chassidy, wait. What did I do?" he asked as he walked toward her.

She turned to him, her face a ball of emotions. "I'm tired of this, Eric. I deserve better."

He reached out to grab her arm. She pulled away.

"I swear to God you'd better not touch me, you jerk! Ayesha can have your trifling behind because I'm done!"

Chassidy walked out of the bedroom and grabbed the bottle of Risata from the countertop before walking out of the palace of faux love. In the hall, she leaned against a wall to gather her thoughts and catch her breath.

In the movies, this would have been the part where the man ran out behind the woman crying, begging, and pleading for a second chance. But in this reality that she had been living for far too long, she knew the only thing Eric truly felt sorry about was that he had been caught. And although Chassidy stood there for a few minutes, he never came after her.

8

The Other Good Wife

***

For the first time in her life Chassidy was thankful for the stop and go traffic of the 405. It meant that Kim couldn't do her usual speeding and dipping in and out of traffic.

Chassidy's nerves wouldn't allow for that following her ordeal with Eric.

After Chassidy left the hotel room, she thought about taking a helicopter ride back to Long Beach, but decided that since Serenity was in good hands and she already had some time off, she would book a room and try to enjoy Catalina.

It had taken her years to actually get there and the weather was perfect. She might as well take advantage of all the island had to offer.

Chassidy knew Eric had returned home the same day she walked out on him because her mother-in-law called to let her know that he had picked up Serenity.

"Is everything alright?" she inquired.

"It isn't, Mrs. Good. I can't do this anymore. I can't take it anymore."

Her mother-in-law didn't try to change her mind. She just listened as Chassidy poured out her heart.

She could hear the hurt in her voice when Mrs. Good said, "I understand, sweetheart. Believe me, I do. Just know that I will always be here for you and Serenity, no matter what."

Chassidy knew that she wholeheartedly meant that and she was comforted by her mother-in-law's encouragement.

Mrs. Good was a woman whose looks betrayed her personality. When Chassidy first met her, she was intimidating—a statuesque and buxom dark-brown woman from the red hills of Mississippi. She was the type of woman who looked like she went to bed in a face full of makeup. Even when she had on rollers and a housecoat her makeup was fresh and she wore her hair in tight roller-set curls every day.

She seemed like the perfect wife and mother—attentive, nurturing, supportive. She prepared three hot meals for her husband every day and never served leftovers. Chassidy wondered how she kept her house so pristine, raised three children, took great care of her husband and played such an active role in her church. Even though she didn't have a conventional job, Chassidy couldn't imagine time enough in the day to do all that she did.

When Chassidy first met Mrs. Good, she saw a look in her eye that would make the average person afraid to cross her. Her hands looked as if she could knock down anyone who stood in her way.

Chassidy later realized that she had a super soft interior and wouldn't dream of hurting a fly, let alone another human being.

A year into Chassidy's marriage, she noticed that everything wasn't as perfect as it seemed. Mr. Good had had multiple outside relationships and Mrs. Good was well aware of them.

Whenever he cheated, she worked even harder to make his home life better for him. She cleaned more, cooked more, and went to church more.

There were even rumors that he fathered a child who lived a few houses down, but Mr. Good denied the accusations and refused to have a blood test.

The more Chassidy got to know Mrs. Good the more she identified the despair that was permanently etched on her face. She could see just how small her mother-in-law felt. She recognized the hopeless and helpless look in her eyes, hidden beneath a smile that lacked any semblance of true joy.

She empathized with her—a traditional woman who didn't know life apart from her marriage. Chassidy was determined not to become *that* woman.

"I still can't believe Eric," Kim said, after Chassidy recapped her weekend. "I swear if I wasn't saved I would put a couple holes in that negro."

"You? It's only by the grace of God he's still living and I'm not locked up somewhere with cornrows and an orange jumpsuit. I'm just saying."

"Do women really wear orange jumpsuits in prison?"

"You know, that's a good question," Chassidy said. "I honestly have no idea. I mean, they do in all the movies, but I don't know."

"Well if they do I definitely couldn't put any holes in him because orange isn't my color. Now give me a royal blue romper with some stilettos and I could do it... Well, if I could still wear my weave, lashes, and get my weekly wax and mani pedis."

There was a brief moment of silence.

Chassidy imagined her friend locked up and flirting with the prison guards while trying to get special treatment. She looked over at her and could tell that Kim had definitely taken a trip to la-la land herself.

There was no telling what she was thinking about but her face said it was naughty.

Kim seemed to snap out of her trance and looked over at Chassidy. They both fell out laughing.

"Kim, you are too much. None of whatever was just going on in that head of yours is actually going to happen, so we'd better just try to keep you out of the system. I'll be alright," Chassidy said.

"Oh, I know you will. You ain't got any other choice."

"Thanks for letting Serenity and me crash at your place for a few nights. I really don't want to fool with Eric right now."

"Girl, please. I understand and you are welcome to stay with me as long as you need."

"I appreciate it," Chassidy said as reality hit her.

Her marriage was over.

Chassidy sighed a wiped a tear from her eye.

"It's gonna be alright," Kim said.

"It hurts so bad."

"I know. But it's gonna feel so good once you completely let go. You deserve better, and honestly, anything is better than everything Eric put you through."

"Yeah."

Chassidy looked out the window as they slowly inched along the freeway. She looked at the faces of drivers in the cars around them. One particular lady looked to be enjoying her time in traffic. Her long blond tresses hung messily below her shoulders. Her music played loudly in her Nissan Dotson. Her windows were rolled all the way down and she sang at the top of her lungs, not seeming to care who could hear the off-tune notes she belted out. She hit her steering wheel and bobbed her head to Alicia Keys.

In another lifetime she would have been a hippie. Something about her apparent freedom settled Chassidy's spirit.

The lady glanced at Chassidy and smiled, revealing a gap the size of a missing tooth. Chassidy was initially shocked and then returned her smile with a heartfelt one of her own.

Yeah. Everything was going to be alright.

9
Stress Relief

* * *

The past week had been a lot more emotionally draining than Chassidy imagined. Staying with Kim was an adjustment. When it came to nights on the town, Kim was smooth. She was always well put together and the average person would assume by looking at her that she lived in a Beverly Hills high rise with servants at her beck and call.

That wasn't the case at all.

She made enough money to hire someone to clean her house every week, but she preferred to use that money to fund the life she lived away from home.

Chassidy didn't consider herself an OCD type, but she did like her space to be tidy and she kept her own home fairly clean.

Little things about Kim's housekeeping were irritating to her. For example, Kim would squeeze toothpaste in the sink and not wipe it up.

Kim also didn't mind leaving a few dirty dishes in the sink at night as long as they were rinsed out.

Chassidy had been raised not to leave a single dish in the sink at night. Kim would read magazines in the living room and then leave them sitting around. The magazines in Chassidy's home were always put back neatly on the coffee table after she finished reading them.

Chassidy tried to straighten things up for Kim each day after work, but the following evening when Chassidy returned from work and picking up Serenity, the same mess would reappear and frustrate Chassidy all over again.

She was thankful for her friend allowing her to crash on her pull-out couch, but she knew she needed to figure out a more permanent living situation for Serenity and herself sooner rather than later.

Kim suggested she return home and make Eric figure out other living arrangements the way normal women did, but too many painful memories greeted Chassidy whenever she thought of their home in Carson. She wanted to get away from it all and was willing to walk away if it meant that she might be able to find a more peaceful place with positive energy.

Chassidy blew out the lavender candle that had been burning on the coffee table and laid down next to Serenity. Her baby girl was so beautiful.

So precious. So innocent.

She hated that she hadn't been able to protect her from the inevitable heartache that came when parents decided they couldn't stand each other and would rather be apart. She hoped Serenity would eventually understand that even though life had pulled her and Eric in two different directions neither of them loved her any less.

She was Chassidy's world, and she knew beyond a doubt that Serenity meant just as much to Eric.

Chassidy remembered when her own parents had split when she was a child. Actually, it was more like her father just left one day and forgot to come back.

She remembered her mother calling the few friends and family they had and asking if anyone had seen him. Afraid that he was laying in an alley somewhere sick or dead, Chassidy's mom strapped Chassidy into the front seat of their Datsun and drove around his old hangout spots looking for him.

Her initial searching and inquiries didn't turn up anything. It was like he had vanished into thin air.

The uncertainty and angst of the first few months was something Chassidy wouldn't wish on her worst enemy. All she knew was that she loved her father and she wanted him to come home more than anything else. She would never forget the look of pity people gave her and her mother whenever they came around. Chassidy's mother finally found out through a friend of a friend that her father was alive and well.

He had picked up and moved to Arizona to be with an older woman he was also dating. Chassidy, like her mother, was heartbroken when she learned the news.

Chassidy didn't see her father again until years later when she was in high school. One day after school she walked into her living room and there he sat with a smile like a Cheshire cat plastered across his face. His arms were extended toward her. Chassidy looked at her mother for a hint about how she should take his return. Her mother smiled and nodded. Chassidy dropped her backpack and rushed into her father's embrace.

Tears streamed down her face as he kissed her forehead and told her that he loved her.

Oh how she had longed to hear those words.

Things seemed to go well for about a week and then, the same as before, he picked up one day and left. Chassidy relived the pain all over again and watched as her mother slowly started to deteriorate mentally, physically, and emotionally.

Chassidy prayed that if ever God blessed her to be a mother that she would also be a wife. In her mind, the unfortunate situation she grew up in was caused by the fact that her mother and father were never married. They dated. They shacked. But her father had never given her mother an official title.

He had never made their relationship official and that was why it was so easy for him to walk away.

It took growing up and living a little to learn that the title didn't always hold the same weight for both people in a marriage—that just because a woman or man had a title, it didn't mean that a marriage would be successful. It didn't mean that you didn't have to worry about someone walking away whenever things got difficult.

Chassidy's mind drifted to Donovan. It had been a couple weeks since she had heard from him. The last time they spoke she came clean and told him about her relationship with Eric—that they had married for Serenity's sake, that they had been in a bad place for years, and that he was finally coming around and trying to make things work.

She told him that she would never forgive herself if she didn't give her marriage one last chance.

Donovan said he understood. He wished her the best but also told her that he would be waiting to hear from her should things not pan out the way she hoped.

Lying in bed now she wondered if it would even be worth it to get to know him better. He looked too good and had too much swag to be a one-woman type of man. She thought back to the night they met.

He assured her that the woman he was with was just a friend. But what if he had been dishonest.

Chassidy didn't want to share a man ever again. Maybe if she didn't expect too much from him he wouldn't be able to break her heart.

Honestly, she was just getting out of a long relationship—a marriage—and even though it had been doomed from the start, she technically needed time to heal the parts of herself that were broken.If she approached Donovan as a stress relief instead of as her knight in shining armor who would walk her down the aisle sometime within the next six months, there was absolutely no way she could get hurt.

Chassidy picked up her phone and clicked on her contacts. She typed in his name. She looked at the time—10:10pm. It was late, but not too late for stress relief.

Hey you, she texted.

Before she could worry about what he might be doing or who he might be with, he texted back, *Hey, sexy. I didn't expect to hear from you so soon.*

Long story, she wrote.

I'd love to hear it. What are you doing right now?

Right now, right now? she asked.

Yeah.

Just thinking about you, she responded.

I want to see you.

I have my daughter with me, but I'm sure I can get a sitter. Where do you want to meet?

Donovan didn't respond right away, but when he did his message said, *There's a movie theatre on Rosecrans. Meet me there at 11:15. There's a movie starting at 11:30. Afterward we can grab a bite.*

Chassidy thought about it for a moment. It was Thursday and she would have to be up bright and early for work the next day, but she really wanted to get out of the house. She really wanted to spend time with Donovan and see if he was worth all the thought she had given him over the past few weeks.

She was sure Kim would be happy to keep an ear out for Serenity. In fact, she'd been encouraging Serenity to call Donovan—or anyone for that matter—since the day she picked her up from the dock in Long Beach.

It was late at night for a date to just be getting started, but what did she have to lose?

Are you still there? Donovan asked.

I'm here. I'll see you at 11:15.

He sent her a meme of a smiling Eddie Murphy from *Coming to America.*

See you soon, sexy lady.

Chassidy eased out of bed and walked down the hall to run her plan by Kim. She could tell that Kim was beyond excited to think of her friend spending time with the fine man from the club.

Kim dug in her nightstand drawer and offered Serenity a handful of condoms.

"What are these for?"

"It's always better to be safe than sorry."

"I don't need these."

"You might."

"Plus, what kind of woman takes condoms on her first date?"

"A woman who knows what she wants," Kim stated matter of factly. "Take it from me, at times like these where your hormones are raging and you haven't released in a while, it is best to have protection with you just in case. And Donovan is fine! I'm almost certain he will get the drawls tonight."

"Whatever," Chassidy said as she took the foil packets from Kim. "I think you're wrong, but I'll take them just in case."

"Thank you."

"Alright, well I'm gonna shower and head out."

"Do you need me to take Serenity to school in the morning?" Kim teased.

Chassidy laughed. "I should be back by 2...3 at the latest."

Kim didn't look convinced. "I'm just saying. Let me know if you need me to take Serenity. I don't have to be at the shop tomorrow until noon, so it won't be a problem."

"I'll keep that in mind," Chassidy said. "And thank you."

"Of course! Anything for you!" Kim said.

Chassidy could hear her singing sexual healing as she headed to the bathroom. She shook her head and chuckled.

That girl is a fool.

10

Any time, Any place

✳ ✳ ✳

Chassidy sat anxiously in her car and waited for Donovan to arrive. The parking lot was fairly empty so she figured she would see him when he pulled up. She gave herself a look in the mirror. She could see a twinge of sadness in her eyes.

Chassidy hoped her time with Donovan would make it disappear. She added a touch more Mac Russian Red lipstick to her peckers and sighed.

This was the first date she had been on in years. She hoped the dating scene was more pleasant to her this time around than it had been to her in the past.

Her relationships had been filled with lies, deceit, distrust, and even verbal abuse on a couple of occasions. Then physical abuse was added into the equation after she married Eric. She shook her head at the thought of it all.

For the most part her relationships had been great in the beginning but quickly spiraled out of control. Perhaps it was because she and her suitors had been so young. They had all just been testing the waters to figure out who they were and what they liked. Maybe if they had met a little later in life things would have turned out differently.

Chassidy was sure that a few of them had gone on to become really good partners and fathers.

To waste a little time and calm her nerves, Chassidy scrolled through her Facebook feed. Her newsfeed usually helped her see the bright side of her own situation.

Scrolling through her feed tonight proved to be a mistake because she noticed that Eric had already changed his relationship status from "Married" to "It's Complicated."

What a jerk.

He could have at least given her the decency to announce their split since he was the one who had ruined everything. She knew the texts from both well-wishers and those who had predicted their demise would start rolling in by morning. God, how she hated him.

How could she have ever married a man so heartless? She prayed that Serenity would never know the misery of a loveless marriage.

She thought about texting Eric to let him know just how trifling he was but decided that it would be better to take the high road. One day he would look back and realize just how good of a wife she had been. Chassidy was certain he would never find anyone who was as devoted as she had been.

And, from a superficial perspective, she had always been out of his league. He should have been honored to have her by his side.

Then a new thought popped into her head. In all of her past relationships, *she* was the common denominator. Was *she* purposely making choices to sabotage her happiness? That couldn't be it. *Who would do such a thing?*

Before she wandered too far down that rabbit hole she heard a tapping at her window. Startled, she looked up to see Donovan standing at the driver's side window with a big smile on his face.

Chassidy smiled back at him and took a few quick breaths to gain her composure.

"You scared me," Chassidy said as she got out of the car and fell into his open arms for a long embrace.

With her head pressed to his chest she could hear the even pace at which his heart beat. He couldn't possibly be as nervous as she was.

"Aw, I'm sorry. I thought for sure you saw me when I walked up."

"Nope."

"Well you must have been deep in thought. Care to share?" Donovan asked as he pulled out of their embrace and looked at Chassidy.

It felt like he was looking through her straight to her soul. She wondered if he could tell just how attracted she was to him. Was there any use in playing coy? Had he already determined that she was easy game or did he anticipate a chase?

There was something about him that made her want to tell him everything. She hadn't known him long, but something about his way made her feel like he could be trusted with her heart because he would understand.

"A little of this and a little of that," she responded, "but I was mostly thinking about you and how this movie had better be good. Especially since I got out of a nice warm bed to be here."

"Is that right?"

"That's right," Chassidy said, trying to avoid his knowing eyes.

"Trust me. You're gonna love it," he said as he gave Chassidy a soft peck on her cheek.

Her knees buckled beneath her. Donovan was smooth. She knew in that moment beyond the shadow of a doubt that Kim had been on to something when she handed her that handful of condoms. There was a time in her life when she would have been ashamed of the naughty thoughts she was having—but not tonight. She deserved whatever goodness Donovan had to offer.

They walked hand in hand toward the theatre. Chassidy welcomed the light breeze that brushed across her body.

"So, what are we going to see?" she asked.

"They play black and white movies at the 11:30 showing on the third Thursday of each month. I never know which one they'll play but I always come and see whatever it is."

"So you're an old-school movie lover? That's a first," Chassidy teased.

"I don't know what it is about them."

At the window, Donovan ordered two tickets.

"You want popcorn?" he asked as they stepped into the foyer.

"I want whatever you want," Chassidy said.

She wasn't particularly hungry, but movies without snacks was like a trip to an arcade without money to play the games. You had to have money.

Donovan gave her a flirty look and licked his lips. "*Whatever* I want?"

Chassidy giggled. "You're so silly. You know what I mean."

"I got excited for a second," Donovan teased. "But I know you're a gentle-woman and would never try to take advantage of me on a first date, even if I was more than willing to be taken advantage of, which I am." He batted his eyes like an innocent school boy.

Chassidy couldn't help but laugh at his playful demeanor. The way he talked and moved gave an air of freedom and lightheartedness that she loved.

"You're crazy," she said and playfully hit his chest.

Donovan smiled at her, revealing a small gap between his two front teeth that she hadn't noticed before. It was adorable.

"I'll get us chicken wings and nachos to share. Would you like a martini or a margarita?" Donovan asked.

Chassidy smiled, "I'd like a blended mango margarita."

Donovan placed their order, which included two blended mango margaritas for her and two Coronas with lime for him. Chassidy hadn't expected to drink on their date, but welcomed the alcohol because it would help her relax. It had been a long time since she had been out with a man as fine as Donovan.

Once they walked in and found a cozy seat in the back row, Chassidy realized that although the previews had started, there was only one other couple inside with them. They sat at the other end of the theatre a few rows ahead of them. She looked at Donovan and smiled knowingly.

"I should have known. How many other ladies have you brought here?"

"What do you mean?"

"Black and white movie no one has heard of. 11:30pm. Almost empty theatre. I see what you're up to?"

"What? I just like black and white movies," Donovan said and gave her a huge smile. "I come here every month. All alone."

Chassidy didn't believe a word of it, but she welcomed the intimacy the theatre provided, so she decided to go along with his story.

"Well I feel special," she said.

"Good. Because you are," he said and leaned in to kiss her neck.

His lips felt soft and full against her skin. She could feel her temperature rise. She closed her eyes and let out a soft moan, anticipating where the night was sure to end. If she had any doubt in her mind before this moment, she was certain that she would know Donovan in the most intimate of ways before the night was over. His lips moved from her neck to her lips. He caressed her face as he kissed her slowly, gently. He grabbed her hand and placed it in his lap.

What she remembered from the club had been spot on.

"Look what you did to me," he said.

Donovan's hand was on her leg working its way toward her sweet spot when the concierge arrived with their food. Chassidy was a little embarrassed by how inappropriately she was behaving with random strangers so close by. But there was something about behaving badly in public that aroused her in a way she had never imagined possible.

The concierge, seeming unbothered, placed their food on the table in front of them, tucked his head, and headed out the rear door.

"Don't worry," Donovan whispered into her ear. "They don't come back until after the movie is over."

Chassidy liked the sound of that. She quickly glanced at the couple on the other side of the theatre.

The man's seat was reclined and the woman straddled him, her body leaning forward at a 45-degree angle. A blanket covered their bodies but from their movements, Chassidy could tell that she was putting in serious work.

They didn't seem to care that there were other people around. Something about their rhythm and the naughtiness of the whole night turned Chassidy on even more.

Donovan seemed to sense her readiness.

He moved their food and drinks to the table next to them and kissed Chassidy more ravenously than he had before. He pressed a button that seamlessly reclined her seat. He slipped her shirt over her head and resumed kissing her neck. His tongue sent electric shocks through her entire body.

As he kissed, he unsnapped her bra and his mouth became familiar with her breasts.

Her nipples had been standing at attention since his kiss on her neck in the parking lot and he gently licked and sucked each breast with passionate intensity.

He took his time and every so often he would ask if she liked the way she felt. She would nod or moan to let her know just how satisfied she was.

Donovan was a smooth lover. She hadn't even felt when he slipped her panties off of her but she knew he had because as he softly sucked on her right breast she could feel his fingers assessing and caressing her vagina.

"Oh gawd," she moaned. It was as if her body was in a trance and she loved everything about the way he made her feel.

He ran his tongue over her belly button briefly before kissing her softly between her thighs. It had been so long since Chassidy had been on the receiving end of oral copulation that she nearly lost her mind when his tongue gently licked her clitoris.

She moaned in pleasure and grabbled the back of his head.

"You taste so good," she heard him say as she let out another long, slow moan. She was used to being the one to make a man feel good but she lay paralyzed by all he was doing to please her.

The spontaneity, Donovan's attention to her moans, his knowing exactly what to do and when to do it—those were things she had longed for. And he seemed to enjoy making her feel good.

In fact, Chassidy wasn't exactly sure how long his head had been between her legs but she knew that she had had multiple orgasms before he even entered her. She wasn't sure when the other couple had exited the theatre, but when she happened to think about them and glance in the direction where they had sat, she was surprised to see that they were gone.

The moment Donovan penetrated her Chassidy really lost control. Theirs was a perfect fit. She couldn't contain herself.

"Oh. My. Gawd," she hollered out as she came harder than she ever had. This caused Donovan's movements to intensify. He worked her harder, faster, and she felt another orgasm coming on. He slowed down his movements and took a deep breath.

"You are so darn sexy," he said to her between strokes.

Chassidy held on to his back. "Please don't stop," she whispered.

His movements quickened and soon he moaned with intense pleasure. She could feel an explosion of moisture between her legs just before he collapsed on top of her. She continued to hold on tight.

"You're trying to get me sprung," he finally said as he caught his breath.

Chassidy couldn't find words to express how amazing her body felt. Instead, she softly kissed his ear. His neck. His lips. She could feel his manhood stiffen again.

She looked him in his eyes and smiled.

"Round two?" she asked.

"Hell yeah," he said.

"Let me ride you," Chassidy said.

Donovan immediately switched positions with Chassidy. She reached into her purse for one of the condoms Kim had given her. Things had been so heated earlier that she was certain Donovan hadn't had time to put one on. She knew Kim was going to ask about protection and she needed to be able to say that she had been responsible—even if she was stretching it a little. She peeled back the wrapper and placed it on Donovan.

The second round was as pleasurable as the first one. After they climaxed, Chassidy knew that she was sprung.

11

Five O'Clock in the Evening Somewhere

✳ ✳ ✳

Chassidy lay across Kim's pull-out sofa. Her night out had been amazing, but it didn't make for an early morning. She hadn't felt this exhausted in years. Chassidy's eyes were open and her mind kept telling her to get up, but her body refused to move.

She heard Kim fumble with her keys outside the door before she burst into the living room, a ball of energy.

Thankfully, she had offered to take Serenity to school when she saw that Chassidy was too beat to do it.

"Dang girl. That must have been some good stuff," Kim said as she plopped on the side of the bed and handed Chassidy a Starbucks espresso.

"Girl!" Chassidy said as she set the drink on the glass end table. "I have never in my life...girl! I don't even know what to say."

"Well I know you need to get up from there and get to work."

"I called out. I can't do it today. I need time to recuperate."

"Like that?" Kim said and took a long swig of her macchiato. "Sounds like you can relate to that 'For Free' song by Drake."

Chassidy thought about the lyrics for a minute and then fell out laughing. "That about sums it up. I felt like I owed him my life savings for putting it on me the way he did."

Kim shimmied, "Yas! I know the feeling. You remember Lemural, don't you?"

Sherry Berry

Chassidy rolled her eyes and sighed. "With a beast of a name like that, how could I forget Mr. Belizian Man?"

"Girl, you remember how messed up he had me. It was so good I had to soak in a warm sitz bath afterward."

"That was crazy," Chassidy laughed.

"Yeah. He had such an appetite too. My gawd, he was a freak. That's the only guy that I couldn't hang with no matter how hard I tried. I used to give myself pep talks before I hung out with him. But each time I would go hard, he would go harder. Whew. That man was something else."

"I remember. It was a mess!" Chassidy laughed.

"I was kinda happy when he got deported because I don't think my taddy-boo would have been good for anything if I had continued messing with him."

"You are too much."

"I'm serious, Chassidy. That man was a freak. He was hung like an ogre or some other oversized beast. In a past life I swear he would have been the leader of the Mandingo warriors. Help me, lawd. I broke out in a sweat just thinking about him."

Kim raised her arms and Chassidy could see that large pools of sweat had soaked her blouse.

"Dang. Now I've gotta change. I was looking forward to rocking this shirt to the shop today," Kim said as she set her coffee on the end table and pulled her shirt over her head. She got up and walked toward her bedroom. "I'll be right back."

Chassidy chuckled. Kim was hilarious. Chassidy would never forget how Lemural put it on her best friend back in the day. It was the only time she had ever seen Kim hand over her number one freak card to anyone. Lemural had such an appetite that Kim had started to look burnt out during the three months she was with him. She was always tired and she kept a bag of ice next to her taddy-boo.

If she wasn't icing, she was soaking. His deportation had been the best thing for Kim, really.

After Lemural left, she took the tips he taught her, applied them to her new conquests, and was right back to expressing the confidence she had in her love-making skills before Mandingo Warrior came on the scene and made her question life.

Kim walked back into the living room wearing a crisp floral button down. "Ok, where were we? Yes,

Donovan's fine behind and how you need to pay him for the way he put it on you."

"Why are you so silly?" Chassidy laughed.

Kim's face was serious. She picked up her macchiato and looked Chassidy in the eye. "When you have a man who looks that good and knows how to work what God has blessed him with the way you have just described it to me, you have to strategize...and really strategize good. He knows what he's got and so does every other woman he's ever dealt with. And from the looks of him that night at the club, even women who haven't experienced him have an idea of what he's working with and want a piece of the action, too. You are going to have to pull out the freak you had in you before you laid her to rest and married Eric's mud duck self."

"You know that mud duck is the father of my beautiful daughter—your beautiful god-daughter."

"I'm sorry, but thank God she got her looks from us. You know it could have been disastrous if she had taken after him."

Chassidy laughed, thankful for her friend having her back through so many ups and downs. Kim didn't know just how just how grateful Chassidy was for her friendship.

"Did she do ok with the drop off?"

"Of course. She was with her Aunt Kim. You know I let her sing as loud as she wanted and gave her tons of candy to distract her."

"Wait. What? You gave her—"

"Relax. I don't get to take my goddaughter to school often. I needed things to go smoothly. And honestly, it's the teacher who will have to deal with the sugar rush. Not us," Kim raised her hand to high five Chassidy, but Chassidy shook her head instead.

"I don't know how I put up with you," Chassidy sighed.

"You're welcome. I can pick her up this afternoon if you need."

Chassidy didn't even give thought to the idea. "Thanks, but no thanks."

"You know I'm messing with you. I just gave her a small piece of peppermint. I mean, even though I don't have kids, I know better than to pump them full of candy first thing—"

Before Kim finished her sentence, Chassidy's phone, which sat next to her espresso, began vibrating enthusiastically. She glanced at it and recognized Donovan's number. She looked at Kim and smiled. "It's him. What do I do?"

"Are you kidding me? What has marriage done to you? Answer it!" Kim said. "I'll give you some privacy. But I want to know all the details," she added before heading down the hallway toward her bedroom.

Chassidy giggled. She cleared her throat and answered like she was full of energy instead of laying stretched out on a pull-out bed unable to move from their night of passion.

"What's up, sexy?" he asked.

"Nothin' much. I was just about to hop in a warm bubble bath and—Wait. Who is this?" Chassidy joked.

"*Who is this?* Oh I see how it is. I haven't been able to get you off my mind and you don't recognize my voice? You don't even have a brotha's number programmed in your phone? It's like that?" Donovan asked playfully.

Chassidy blushed. She hadn't been able to get him off her mind either. "Is this the fine chocolate brotha that took me to a black and white movie that I can't even remember the name of because we were so busy getting busy that we didn't see any of it?"

Donovan laughed heartily, "You're wild, girl. You had me nervous for a while."

"Donovan, we both know that you're not the type to easily be forgotten."

"Is that right? I wish I could join you in that warm bubble bath."

"I wish you could too."

"I can easily make that happen. What's your address?"

Chassidy laughed nervously. "You know I'm at my girl Kim's house. I can't just be inviting people into her home like that."

"I'm not just 'people' though. I'm trying to be your man."

Chassidy felt a chill run through her body. Even though she didn't know him well enough to honestly consider making him her man, she liked the sound of that.

"Oh really?" she asked. "I'll tell you what. Give me five minutes and I'm gonna FaceTime you. It will be just like we're together."

"Not *just* like," Donovan said. She imagined him licking his lips.

She thought about it for a moment. "You're right. It won't be just like, but it will be fun."

Donovan paused for a moment. "The only thing is that I'm gonna have to see you today—and the sooner the better."

"Well you're in luck. I took the day off, so that won't be a problem at all."

"Bet," Donovan said. "Alright. Well I'll call you in ten."

Once Chassidy sat the phone down she realized that just the sound of his voice had made her moist. She got up, straightened up the living room, and placed her espresso in the refrigerator. She grabbed her phone, a glass, and a bottle of moscato and headed toward the bathroom. It was 9 am in Los Angeles, but, hell, it was 5 o'clock in the evening *somewhere*.

Chassidy tapped on Kim's door and peeped her head in. "Kim, I'm about to get a bath and head out. If the offer still stands—"

"Don't worry. I'll pick her up. Have fun," Kim returned.

Chassidy thanked her and headed to the bathroom for the type of action Syleena Johnson and Twista describe in their collaboration "Phone Sex."

There was a time Chassidy would have been too reserved to do something so naughty in her best friend's bathroom, but with Donovan was on the scene, that time was gone.

While she filled the tub, she poured a glass of wine and ran to the living room to grab the water-friendly bullet she had tucked in her duffle bag for such a time as this. Minutes ago, she had been exhausted. Now she was wide awake with anticipation. This was going to be good!

12

The Windows Got Foggy
✳ ✳ ✳

Who knew that two full-grown adult bodies could melt together so perfectly in the passenger's seat of a Nissan Sentra? If someone had told Chassidy that it was possible before today she would have seriously doubted it.

Being parked at the Culver City scenic outlook with the seat leaned all the way back and Donovan having just given her one of the most powerful orgasms she had ever experienced, she was now a believer. With the exception of the front one, Donovan had limo tint on the windows.

When they first parked he put a sun visor on the front window and things got pretty heated from there. He left the car running and the air pumping for the half hour they made love.

During the final minutes Chassidy could see in his eyes that he was about to erupt. She leaned forward, her right knee digging into the middle console, and gyrated slowly on top of him.

Donovan squeezed her behind tightly and gave it a good smack. He moaned. Soon his body pumped wildly beneath her and she picked up her pace as well. She moaned her satisfaction and he hollered out in pleasure.

Once he climaxed, she did a few Kegels and a few more soft strokes before collapsing onto him.

He held her in a gentle embrace while they both caught their breath.

"Sorry I came so fast," Donovan panted. "I couldn't help myself."

Chassidy blushed and giggled as she moved a stray curl out of her face. "I came a couple times myself... before we even got started," she admitted.

"Dang. Like that?"

Chassidy looked at Donovan with a naughty look in her eye. She nodded and gently bit and then kissed his bottom lip. "I'm not embarrassed about it though. You've got just what my body needs."

Donovan kissed Chassidy on the neck, sending thrills through her body once again.

She melted back into an embrace and they held each other. They didn't speak for the next few moments. Chassidy thought about how much she liked this man and felt a little guilty because she knew so little about him.

Was he born and raised in Los Angeles? Did he believe in God? Did he have a degree? Children? Siblings? Had he ever been married? How long was his longest relationship? Where did he work? Where did he live? Hell, what was his FICO score? Chassidy didn't know any of the answers.

As if he could sense the questions swirling around in her mind he said, "How would you like to grab a bite and talk?"

"I'd really like that, actually," she smiled.

"Good. I have a couple hours before I have to get back to work, so we should be good. Have you ever been to The Serving Spoon?"

"I have not, but I hear their chicken and waffles are really good."

"They are," Donovan affirmed. "Alright, well that's where we'll go."

Chassidy lifted up so he could pull up and zip his pants. She put her panties back on and adjusted her skirt. Once they were decent, Donovan got out of the car and headed back to the driver's side. He removed the visor and they headed toward Inglewood.

13

Be My Girl

✳ ✳ ✳

"This is really good, D," Chassidy said as she took another bite of her cinnamon sprinkled waffle. "It's like a little bit of heaven."

Donovan laughed, "Is it that good?"

"It really is. Your omelet looks amazing and I'm not even an egg lover."

"It is," Donovan said as he took a bite. "They kill it every time. This is one spot that never lets me down."

"Well, I'll definitely be back. It's crazy because when I see mom and pop restaurants I never think to go in, but every so often someone recommends one that winds up on my list of favorites."

"Yeah. I love finding the best when and where I least expect it. It's kinda like the night I met you."

"Really?" Chassidy teased and took a sip of her coffee. "How is that so?"

"My homegirl was having a rough time and I thought a night out would cheer her up. Liquor and music always do it for me," he smiled.

"I'll be sure to remember that," Chassidy said flirtingly.

"There are a lot of things that do it for me. Music and liquor are just two of them," he said naughtily. "But don't worry, you've got most of the other things on my list checked off, too."

Chassidy shifted in her seat and grinned. She wondered what all was on his list. What was she lacking? What did she already possess?

"Anyway," Donovan continued, "when I saw you, I felt a connection like I've never felt before and it wasn't just physical. I hoped you felt something too because I had a strong desire to get to know you better."

"I felt the same way," Chassidy admitted. "But I really thought you and your homegirl were together and trying to recruit me for a kinky threesome."

Donovan laughed so hard that quite a few patrons looked at him to see what was so funny. Not seeing anything, they smiled and went back to eating their meals. Donovan's laugh was so hearty and sincere that Chassidy couldn't help but laugh, too.

"Naw," Donovan finally said, "Trina is really just my homegirl. Nothing more and nothing less—unless you want a kinky threesome. I might be able to make that happen," he said and laughed.

Chassidy gave him a side eye and shoed his hand, "Boy, bye! I am not the one for that."

"I know, I know. I'm just messing with you."

"Have you two ever messed around? I mean, you seemed pretty close that night."

Donovan took another bite of his omelet and swallowed it down before he spoke. The pause made Chassidy feel nervous about what he would say next.

"Let me say this, you have nothing to worry about. Trina isn't my type. We did mess around a few times when we were younger, but we realized we could never work in a real relationship."

"Why not?" Chassidy asked.

Donovan appeared to mull over the question.

Finally, he spoke, "Well, me not being attracted to her is a big one. I don't think I could be faithful to someone I'm not attracted to."

"Really?" Chassidy asked. She was surprised by his honesty, but she loved it.

"Really. I know I'm a good looking man. I've been told that my whole life. I also know what type of woman I can pull—what type of woman I see myself with—and she's just not it. She's a nice girl, but she's not the one."

That was so blunt that it hurt Chassidy's feelings on Trina's behalf.

"Have you ever told her that?" Chassidy asked.

"Trina's my friend. She knows what's up."

Chassidy took a sip of her coffee and looked at all the picture frames that hung on the walls. "A lot of celebrities and politicians have eaten here. I can't believe I've been sleep on this place for so long."

Donovan touched Chassidy's hand and her eyes met his.

"I'm attracted to you though," he said, "and I would love to be more than just your friend."

Chassidy's heart raced. He was so fine. And the way he said that sounded so good.

"I would like that very much, but you know my situation."

"I don't care about your situation. It's temporary," Donovan said. "I want you to permanently be my girl."

She laughed nervously. "Seriously? I feel like you just handed me a paper that says 'will you go with me' and you want me to circle yes or no."

Donovan smiled, "That's exactly what I want you to do—circle yes or no."

Chassidy thought about it for a moment. She really liked Donovan but she was old enough to know not to jump into a relationship with a man she barely knew. Jumping into one with one she knew had proven disastrous.

"Look, I think we should take time to get to know each other a little more."

"I know enough about you," Donovan protested.

"What's my last name?"

"Good."

"No, my maiden name?"

Silence.

"When is my birthday?"

Silence.

"Am I originally from California?"

"No."

"Actually, the answer is yes. What's my favorite color?

Silence.

"What college did I attend and what was my major?"

Silence.

The look on Donovan's face also showed that he understood where Chassidy was coming from.

"Look D, I like you. It's strange because I don't know any of those answers about you either, but I like you a lot. I want to spend more time with you. I want to get to know you better. I'm good with that now—getting to know you better and possibly working toward a relationship *if* we're compatible."

"See that's why I like you so much. You're right. We can take our time. I already know I want to be with you and you're gonna like me even more once you get to know me. It's a win-win."

Chassidy smiled. She hoped he was right.

"So are you talking to other people," Donovan asked as he tried to sound nonchalant.

"No one but you," Chassidy said.

"Good. I don't want to share you."

"You do realize that I'm still married, right?"

"That's over. He's a non-factor. I don't want to share you, Chassidy. Promise me you won't give your stuff away to anyone but me."

Chassidy shifted in her seat. She hadn't had a conversation like this one since college. She had been off the dating scene for a while but she thought she had aged out of this foolishness. She thought relationships and monogamy and things of that nature just came naturally.

No questions asked.

Perhaps that had been the reason things hadn't worked out up until this point.

This was different, but she figured she'd ride with it. It couldn't hurt to lay out the parameters early on.

"I'm a one-man kind of woman," Chassidy said.

Donovan seemed to relax. "If I'm talking to you, I'm talking to you. Right now, you're the only man I'm talking to. If anything changes I'll let you know, but I don't expect it to change because I like you."

Chassidy took a sip of her drink before asking the question that had been on her mind as well. "How about you? Will you be sharing all that goodness with anyone else?"

"I'm all yours as long as you'll have me," he said with a coy smile.

14

Home Sweet Home
✳ ✳ ✳

Chassidy looked around her new apartment and exhaled. It had taken her a couple of uncomfortable months on Kim's couch before she found a place in Playa Vista that was just right for Serenity and her. Two bedrooms, two bathrooms, 980 square feet, washer and dryer in unit, access to swimming pools, BBQ pits, the clubhouse, and the building's gyms for $3,000 a month.

It was much pricier than the mortgage she and Eric shared, but peace of mind was worth it. Even though Chassidy had some money saved it would be tight each month paying her rent, car note, and other expenses, but she would figure out how to make it all work. This place was the perfect place to keep her spirits up in spite of the unfortunate turn her marriage had taken. Her salary and savings along with the money she received each month from Eric would be enough to finance her decisions.

Chassidy couldn't sleep, so she poured herself a glass of warm milk, plopped down on her leather sofa, and turned to the U-Verse jazz station. So much was going on that she hardly had a chance to breathe. She was bogged down with searching for the perfect apartment, moving, and trying to be out of her feelings enough to co-parent with a man who was moving on with multiple women since their split. Not to mention figuring out how she would financially support Serenity, trying to protect Serenity's little heart as much as possible, being present at work through all the drama, adjusting to life as a single mother, and dating a man who was fine as hell but M.I.A. a little too much for comfort. Her period was a couple weeks late, but she was certain it was because of all the duress she was under. It was all so overwhelming.

It was almost midnight and she hoped the warm milk and music would relax her enough to finally get some rest. She had a long day ahead of her, but she couldn't stop thinking about Donovan and the rollercoaster they had been on over the past few weeks.

When she was with him things were great. He was super attentive and it felt like she was the only woman in the world. He opened car doors, kept her laughing, and romanced her like crazy. They conversed about important things like religion, politics, the state of the Black man in America, and institutionalized racism in banking and real estate. They talked about silly things like which Wayans brother was the most successful or which housewife had the most money. They made plans for a future together. They talked about when it would be the right time for him to meet Serenity. They even discussed him possibly moving in in a few months.

The talks were amazing, but it didn't take Chassidy long to notice that he was available during the week but seemed to disappear Friday afternoon through Monday morning. He gave excuses that made Chassidy feel like he thought she was stupid.

One weekend, he said he had lost his phone. The next, it had fallen in the toilet and when he switched it out all his contacts had been erased. Another weekend, he said he had gone to Vegas with friends but his phone plan didn't cover him outside of California. All his excuses were suspect—the equivalent of a high school student saying his dog ate his homework—but he had always seemed so honest when they were together that Chassidy overlooked his absences.

A few days ago, Donovan surprised her. Their conversation had gone something like this:

"This weekend I want you to meet my mom and sister."

Chassidy pulled the phone away from her ear and checked to make sure she was indeed on the phone with Donovan. It was him alright. She didn't quite know how to respond. With the exception of the night they met, she had never spent time with him on the weekend and meeting his family, who he talked so much about, was a big deal.

"Seriously?" Chassidy asked. "This weekend?"

"Yeah. I think it's time. Especially since we're planning to be together. They need to meet the special woman in my life.

Chassidy smiled. "Me?"

"Yeah you, sexy. I told them that I plan to marry you one day."

Chassidy blushed. She felt bad for ever feeling like Donovan was playing her for a fool. For him to introduce her to the most important people in his life meant that he was serious about her.

"Are you still there?" Donovan asked.

"I'm here," Chassidy said. "I'd love to meet them. Just tell me the time and place and I'll be there."

"I'll pick you up Saturday afternoon around 12," Donovan said.

Chassidy was nervous. She couldn't believe that in a few short hours she would meet them. Donovan had told her that his family was bourgeois and didn't like any of his exes but he assured her that they would love her because she was a classy woman. She hoped he was right.

Chassidy had just taken a deep breath when she heard the patter of little feet walking down the hallway.

"Mommy," Serenity whined. "I can't sleep."

"Aw, baby. What's the matter?" Chassidy asked as she set her milk on the coffee table and sat her precious little lady on her lap.

"I had a bad dream," Serenity said and buried her head in her mother's chest.

Chassidy rubbed her curly auburn mane and kissed the top of her head.

"It's ok, baby girl. I'm here. I won't let anyone hurt you."

"When are we going home, Mommy?" Serenity asked. "I miss my real room."

Chassidy could feel a familiar pain in her chest and lump in her throat.

"Aw, baby girl, remember Mommy told you that this our new home now? You can still spend time in your old room and in your old bed when you're with your dad, but while you're with me you have a really nice princess bed and beautiful room that you helped me decorate. Remember?"

Serenity's whimpers turned into full on sobs.

"I miss Daddy."

Chassidy held her tighter in her arms and silently shed a few tears along with her daughter. She could only imagine how hard this was for her. It hurt like hell to know there was nothing she could do to take away her daughter's pain.

"It's going to be alright, baby girl. I promise."

Neither of them said another word for what felt like an eternity. Finally, Serenity asked, "Do you love Daddy?"

Chassidy thought about it for a moment and tapped into her biblical repertoire for what she said next. "Of course I do, baby girl. I love everybody and I will always love your father."

"Will you ever stop loving me?"

Chassidy pulled her daughter away from her chest and looked her squarely in the eyes. "Of course not! I will never ever stop loving you. You are my heart."

"I love you too, Mommy."

Chassidy smiled and gave her another tender kiss on the top of her head.

"Do you want to tell me about your dream?"

Serenity paused and then nodded. "I dreamed that I forgot to put my dolls away and you and Daddy were yelling at each other and then he called me a bad girl and then you told me you didn't love Daddy anymore and that you didn't love me either." As she relayed her dream she sniffled and Chassidy's heart ached.

"Aw, sweetheart. That sounds like a horrible dream. Your Daddy and I both love you more than anything else in this world. You are such a good and precious little girl and neither of us will ever stop loving you, okay?"

Serenity nodded her head, "Okay, Mommy."

"Do you want to sleep with me tonight?"

Serenity nodded her head.

"Okay. We can sing songs and I'll read you a story. Would you like that?"

Serenity nodded.

"Okay," Chassidy said as she picked up Serenity and turned off the television.

She rinsed out her glass and with Serenity still on her hip she flipped off the dim light in the living room and headed down the hallway to snuggle with the love of her life.

15

Meet the Parent

✳ ✳ ✳

"That's it," Donovan said as he slowed in front of a modest, ranch-style home on a tree-lined street surrounded by other homes just like it. "That's where I grew up."

Chassidy took a deep breath, hoping it would help her relax. It looked like a very cozy home, but she noticed that that there were quite a few people, dressed to the nines (and mostly in black), standing in front of it and there wasn't a single parking space on the immediate block.

"You didn't mention a party," Chassidy said as she looked down at her jeans jeggings, beige turtle neck, and over-the knee flat brown boots. "I feel underdressed." She glanced at Donovan, who was dressed up more than usual—black slacks, black shirt, black tie, black Stacy Adams. How had he missed giving her the all-black memo?

Donovan rubbed her leg. "It's not really a party," Donavan said. "My stepdad passed away and today was his funeral."

"What? Oh my gawd, are you kidding me right now? Your stepdad?" Chassidy asked incredulously. "So you brought me here for a funeral?"

"Not exactly. The funeral was this morning. This is the repass."

Chassidy couldn't believe it. Her first time meeting Donovan's family would be at a repass. This was her first time hearing about him having a stepfather and Donovan hadn't mentioned his passing before today. What kind of person would introduce this family to a love interest at a repass? And even more of a quagmire was why Donovan thought it ok to put her in such an uncomfortable situation without running it by her first.

"Well, this is pretty awkward."

"It will be fine. Trust me," Donovan said as he drove to the next block and parked.

Perhaps this was a difficult time for Donovan. Maybe he was one of those people who didn't know how to handle pain and loss. Maybe he needed her for moral support but hadn't known the right words to say to ask for it. Still, this whole situation crossed so many lines on so many levels. She imagined his mother and sister would feel the same.

"Well—I'm sorry for your loss," Chassidy said tenderly enough to betray her indignation.

"Thanks, but I'm good. We never really got along. I know my mom and sis are going through it though."

"I bet," Chassidy said, still trying to make sense of it all. "So you missed the funeral?"

"I don't do funerals."

Donovan reached for his dark sunglasses. "Are you ready?" he asked.

"No," Chassidy said. "Why did you bring me here today?"

"I want my family to meet you. Everyone is here."

"I just don't think this is the appropriate time or place."

"Don't worry, Chas. They're going to love you. They're going to know how special you are because I brought you with me. Just trust me. It will be fine.

Follow my lead." He gave her a slow, soft kiss on her cheek. She felt her usual butterflies.

Chassidy shook her head. None of this made any sense, but she really did care about Donovan. If this was what he wanted her to do and if this was how he wanted her to do it, she would put on her best mourning face and make it happen for her man. Perhaps she would understand it all better by the time they left.

He was out of the car and at Chassidy's door in a flash. He opened it and helped her out.

"Just trust me," he said again.

Chassidy nodded and they walked hand in hand toward his mother's home.

The day trudged along. Chassidy felt extremely out of place as Donovan conversed with family and friends. He always made a point to introduce her as his future wife, but no one looked as if they believed him. They smiled politely and either continued talking with Donovan or moved on to the next. Donovan's mother and sister seemed kind, considering the circumstances, but neither of them went out of their way to make Chassidy feel like she would soon be welcome in their family.

Chassidy sat alone in the den somewhat watching whatever was on HGTV while Donovan talked with some of his uncles in the living room. The den provided just the solitude Chassidy needed to take her mind off the busyness in the rest of the house. She had been in there for a while when the most gorgeous little girl, who appeared to be around five years old, walked in and smiled at her. It was the first genuine smile she had seen from anyone other than Donovan since they arrived two hours ago.

"Hi, pretty girl. What's your name?"

The little girl's eyes had a familiar sparkle.

"I'm Donyel," she said and extended her hand for a shake."

"Danielle?" Chassidy asked as she shook her hand.

"No. Don-yel," she said with a smile. Her deep dimples and the small gap between her teeth were adorable. She wore two long braided ponytails that made her look like she was mixed with Native American.

"Donyel. That's a pretty name."

"Thank you," she blushed and sat next to her on the plastic covered sofa.

They talked for a few minutes. Chassidy learned that Donyel was indeed five. She was in kindergarten and attended Coliseum Street School, which was right around the corner. She said that Donovan's mom, whom she affectionately called Big Momma, watched her every day after school until her mother, Daniella, picked her up in the evenings. Daniella and Donovan's sister, whom Donyel referred to as Auntie, were best friends. It was evident that Donyel was a very bright, sweet, and outspoken little girl who had a special relationship with the family.

Donovan peeked his head in the door and made a face Chassidy had never seen him make when he saw Donyel next to her.

"What are you doing in here?" he asked.

"I'm talking to Ms. Chassidy," she replied sweetly.

"Well, go talk to your mom. She's looking for you."

"Ok, Mr. Man," Donyel giggled as she rolled her eyes and scurried out of the room.

"Why'd you make her leave me, D?" Chassidy asked as soon as she was out of sight. "I was having a good time talking with her."

Donovan walked over to Chassidy and plopped down on the couch next to her.

"She acts too grown," Donovan said. "And her mom is always looking for somebody else to do for her daughter what she should be doing. I can't stand women like that."

"Well, it seems to me she is a very well-mannered little girl. And she is adorable! I think Serenity would love hanging out with her. Maybe one day, after the two of you meet, we can stop by for a playdate."

"That will *never* happen," Donovan said, with annoyance in his voice. "I don't even come over here that much because Donyel and her mom are always here. My peeps treat them better than they do me."

Chassidy knew Donovan was a little jealous, but seeing his reaction to Donyel and her mother didn't sit well with her. Perhaps the circumstances of their being there was getting to him more than he cared to admit.

Chassidy rubbed his back but didn't respond. Before she knew it, tears were streaming down his face. She gave him a few tissues from the box on the coffee table in front of them. He wiped his eyes and leaned his head back.

"I hated that man, Chassidy," Donovan said. She could feel the intensity in his voice.

She continued to rub his back, "It's alright. Let it out," Chassidy said tenderly.

"He used to tell me I wasn't worth a damn and that I would never be a real man like he was. And he used to beat my behind. Man, did he beat my behind. My sister never seemed to do anything wrong, and my mother never stood up for me. I thought going off to college and getting my degree would make him respect me. I was wrong."

"And when I moved back here and couldn't find a job after I graduated, he said it was because I had chosen a woman's major. Liberal Arts wasn't a real thing and I wouldn't be able to get a real job with that degree. He complained about all the money they had spent to help me through school and how they had to pay my student loans because my 'lazy behind' wasn't smart enough to get a job."

"I can't tell you how many jobs I applied for or how many rejection emails I received. I tried, but he didn't respect trying. In his mind, I never did enough.

"I was happy when I was finally able to move out on my own. It was a struggle but I did what it took so I wouldn't have to see his face. I was determined to prove him wrong and make him respect me." Donovan looked down and said dejectedly, "Guess that will never happen."

Chassidy could feel the pain coursing through his body with each breath he took. She held him tightly and said softly, "Now, I need you to *trust* me. You are so much more than what he refused to see about you."

"You don't understand," Donovan interrupted.

"No, I really do understand. For years I blamed myself for my father leaving. I thought I wasn't good enough or smart enough or pretty enough to make him want to be around for my mom and me. It hurt like hell to know he was in another state with another woman being a father to her children while my mom and I struggled to get by. I finally realized that my worth has nothing to do with what anybody else thinks or doesn't think about me. It has nothing to do with who chooses to be present in my life or who decides I'm not worth the time. It matters most what God thinks and what I think."

"I'm not trying to sound conceited, but if I'm honest with myself, I've got it going on considering the hand I was dealt. I have a degree from a great school, a beautiful daughter, a good paying job, a nice place to stay, and food to eat. To top it off, I am a good person. What more could I ask for?"

"I didn't hear you mention your man on that list," Donovan joked as he wiped his eyes with the backs of his hands.

"Oh yeah...that part. And I've got the most handsome, hardworking, intelligent, caring, and hilarious man in all of Southern California sitting next to me and telling everyone I'm his future wife. What more could I ask for?"

"That sounds better now," Donovan laughed.

"Seriously though, forget about him and what he could or could not see. He's dead now and his opinion of you never mattered anyway. It matters only what God thinks and what you think of yourself. And as an added bonus, I think the world of you," Chassidy said as she kissed him on the cheek.

"I love you," Donovan whispered.

Chassidy's heart skipped a beat. She held her breath for a moment as the weight of his declaration hit her. She wasn't expecting to hear those words so soon. This would be the perfect time to tell him that she loved him too, but she wasn't sure that her feelings had quite made it to that level. She held Donovan in her arms and pretended she hadn't heard what he said. She hoped he didn't repeat himself—not today anyway.

After a few minutes, Donovan finally said what Chassidy had hoped to hear since they first arrived, "Let's get out of here and do something fun."

"Fun? Does that include something to release this tension?" she asked as she rubbed his thigh.

"I wouldn't have it any other way," Donovan said as he licked his lips. "Look what you did to me," he said with a naughty smile. Chassidy noticed the excited bulge in his pants.

"I see," Chassidy smiled.

"We could just dip into the bathroom for a little while," Donovan suggested as he batted his eyes. "I mean, no one's checking for me and with how I'm feeling right now, all I need is a few minutes."

"What if I need a little more than that?" Chassidy joked.

Donovan gave her a few soft kisses on her neck. Chassidy closed her eyes and let out a soft moan. He did a little trick with his tongue that instantly made her feel down below what he was doing up top.

"I have a feeling you only need a few minutes too," Donovan said.

He was right.

"Follow me," he said as they made their way to a bathroom at the rear of the house.

16

Kiss and Tell... and More
✻ ✻ ✻

"So, you mean to tell me y'all got it cracking in the bathroom at his momma's house while friends and family mourned the loss of his stepfather in the next room?"

Chassidy nodded her head.

Kim put her hand on her chest and gasped.

"Nobody needed to use the bathroom or anything?"

"There were a few knocks but Donovan just told 'em he'd be out soon."

"Y'all are some freaks!" Kim asserted. "How long were y'all in there?"

"First of all, I know you ain't talking," Chassidy laughed. "You must have forgotten that I know all your hoe stories. There's no way I could ever make it to your freak level."

"What?" Kim rolled her eyes. "All I know is that I have *never* had sex at a funeral."

"It wasn't a funeral," Chassidy reminded her. "It was a repass. There's a huge difference."

"Was there a minister in the house?"

Chassidy nodded.

"How about really sad people dressed in all black?"

"Whatever."

"Were they there mourning the loss of someone who had died?"

"Get out of here, Kim," Chassidy laughed.

"I'm just asking. 'Cause it sounds to me like the repass had the same people and things at it that the funeral did. I'm just saying."

"Please don't try to make me feel some kind of way about the amazing love I made in the quarter bathroom in the back of my man's mother's house."

"Wait. You didn't mention it was a tiny bathroom. So there was just a toilet and a sink in there?"

Chassidy nodded her head.

"That's what's up. My man Donovan has unleashed my girl's inner sexual beast! I'm loving this! So I'm guessing you rode him real good."

"You would have been proud," Chassidy confessed.

Kim gave her a high-five as she walked toward the electric coffee pot to pour herself another cup.

"Would you like some?"

"You know, coffee has been making me nauseous lately. Honestly, I can't keep much of anything down before noon. Even water has been giving me problems. It's the strangest thing."

Kim gave her a side eye. "Really? Have you and Donovan been using protection."

"Of course," Chassidy answered a little too quickly.

"Every time?"

"I mean, 99.9 percent of the time. We slipped up that one time at the movies, but that was it."

"Hmm. Well it sounds to me like that .1 percent must be what did it," Kim said as she shook her head and sat back in her seat.

All the color drained from Chassidy's face as the weight of Kim's words hit her. She and Donovan had made a lot of love over the past few months, but they had used protection every time... except the first time.

She could feel her heart racing.

Come to think of it she had indeed missed her period, but she assumed it was because of the stress from the divorce. She had been nauseous and extremely tired for the past month or so.

Now it all made sense. Her heart sank. This couldn't be happening at a worse time. How would it look to be pregnant by a man who wasn't her husband before their divorce was final? She could imagine how pissed Eric would be when she shared the news with him. How would she explain things to Serenity? What would Donovan say?

She cared about him, but she honestly didn't know him well enough to know how he would take the news.

"Why are you so quiet?" Kim asked as she looked Chassidy up and down.

"Well, I have a lot going through my head right now. You might be right. I feel stupid because that never even crossed my mind. I guess I've been too stressed out to think about important stuff like that. I've even had a few glasses of wine over the past few months. That would be horrible if I really am pregnant."

"Well, don't judge me, but I have a test under the bathroom sink. You're welcome to it."

"What? You just keep pregnancy tests around? Why? I thought you don't want kids."

"I don't, but I did have a little scare with that guy Dylan I was talking to a few months ago."

"I remember you saying your period was a little late, but you didn't tell me you bought a test."

"Look, that's neither here nor there. My period came the same day I bought the test, so you didn't miss anything. And now we can find out right now whether or not you're pregnant. It all worked out."

"God, I hope I'm not pregnant. That would just be too much drama and I don't need that right now."

They both sat in silence for a while. Kim took an occasional sip of coffee while Chassidy tried to calm her own nerves.

Finally, Chassidy walked to the bathroom and closed the door behind her.

17

Alright

✳ ✳ ✳

"Pregnant?" Donovan asked as he nervously paced back and forth in Chassidy's living room. "You think it's mine?"

Chassidy was shocked and a little offended by his question for just a second until she remembered that guys normally had questions like that in circumstances like these.

It was the same question Eric had asked when she told him she was pregnant with Serenity. It was the same question she hoped Serenity would never be asked.

Her hope for her daughter was that she would do things in order—meet and fall in love with someone, marry him and *then* have children.

"I'm positive. You remember when I told you that you're the only man I've been romantic with in a long time? I was serious."

Donovan sighed and plopped down on the couch next to her. He didn't say anything for what felt like an eternity. Chassidy tried to read him but couldn't. She rubbed his leg.

"Man," he finally said, defeated. "It was probably that night at the movies."

Chassidy nodded her head. "It must have been."

Donovan stared at the television, which was muted and tuned to ESPN. A few minutes of uncomfortable silence passed.

"So what are you going to do?" he finally asked.

Chassidy took a deep breath.

"That's what I want to talk to you about. I mean, there's just so much going on right now. I'm still married, for Christ's sake. I honestly don't know what to do, but I didn't think it would be fair to make this decision without your input."

Donovan nodded his head. "I appreciate that."

"If I have this baby, I need to know that you're all in because…"

"Let me stop you there," Donovan said as he turned to face Chassidy. "If you are considering what I think, I can tell you that I'm not ready to be a father. I can't tell you what to do with your body, but now really isn't a good time. I care about you a lot, but I would much rather bring a child into the world with you the right way and at the right time. This right here, right now… this isn't right."

Chassidy could see the pleading in his eyes and hear the urgency in his voice. She felt a familiar pain in her chest. She had pondered about the right place and time to break this news to him and she had already played through all his possible responses.

She had considered this one, but she hadn't thought that it would actually hurt as much as it did.

Perhaps it wasn't always the case, but she felt like his response was the one jump-offs across the world received when they had laid with the wrong man and gotten caught up.

"Look baby," he said, "I hope I'm not hurting your feelings. I support whatever you want to do, but I just don't think now is the right time. I want to be your man. I want to be the father of your children, and I'm hoping to have a whole baseball team worth of sons, but I want to be married to you first.

Besides, being pregnant with another man's baby will only complicate things with your divorce."

Chassidy looked into his eyes and could tell that he meant what he was saying.

"I respect that," she said. "And I appreciate your honesty."

"So are you gonna get rid of it?" he asked a little too anxiously.

Chassidy didn't answer right away. She wondered what it was like to choose this route instead of the one where you have the baby and make things work—with or without the involvement of the father. Would this decision be a harder choice to make? Would she ever be able to forgive herself for it? Would God forgive her?

"So, are you going to get rid of it?" Donovan asked again.

"Yeah. I'll see when I can get an appointment to terminate," she said. Her heart dropped again. "Do you think you can be there with me, you know, when I go to the clinic?"

"Just let me know when and I'll do my best to be by your side," Donovan said.

Chassidy put her head on his chest as he held her in his arms. She mourned the son or daughter they would never know. She could hear the rapid beating of Donovan's heart.

He kissed the top of her head.

"It's gonna be alright," he said, seemingly more to himself than to her. He repeated, "It's gonna be alright."

18

Only Brokenhearted
✳ ✳ ✳

Chassidy sat in her office at First Trust Bank and stared out the window, as she had done each day since terminating her pregnancy. Kim suggested she take a little personal time to heal emotionally, but Chassidy preferred being at work than anywhere else.

Although she hadn't accomplished much in the past two weeks, she arrived early and stayed late. Thankfully, she had trained her assistant well enough to keep a handle on her clients and accounts, so there hadn't been any bumps or hiccups to cause them alarm.

She would have to thank Sam with a very nice token of appreciation—maybe an all-expense paid trip to somewhere tropical.

Whatever the cost, Sam was worth it.

Chassidy didn't open up about exactly what was unfolding in her life, but she did tell Sam about the divorce, the move, and the overwhelming feelings of doing so much on her own.

Sam sat and cried with her one day after work, and that meant the world to Chassidy. After that, she would bring Starbucks teas and coffees, gourmet breakfasts and lunches, and anything else she thought would help Chassidy through the process.

"Don't worry, boss," Sam encouraged, "God is in control. My favorite scripture says that all things work together for good to them that love the Lord, to those who are the called according to His purpose. You've got to believe that all of this is happening now so that the better that God has for you can make its way to you."

That scripture had always encouraged Chassidy, but now it reminded her that so much of what she was going through was happening because of poor choices she made. She knew Sam mentioned it because she only knew of the circumstances Chassidy was the victim in. Would she still quote that same verse if she knew about her involvement with Donovan? Would she still quote the same verse if she knew that Chassidy was a murderer? Chassidy broke down even more—and Sam held her in her arms.

"It really will be alright, boss lady."

Chassidy wasn't so sure. She felt like her entire life was falling apart. She hated that she had added the Donovan drama to her already hectic life.

After the night she told Donovan about her pregnancy and agreed to terminate it, their "relationship" really fell apart. He completely went off the grid for a couple of weeks.

She called and texted but didn't hear anything from him until after the procedure was over.

Thankfully, Kim accompanied her to the doctor's office and was there to drive her home and comfort her afterward.

When Donovan's number did appear on her screen, Chassidy answered, ready to fuss about how he had left her hanging, but also content to forgive him and hopefully move forward if that's what he wanted. But the call didn't go as planned.

"*Donovan?*"

"*No, this is his fianceé, Trina. Is this Chassidy?*"

Chassidy's jaw dropped, her head spun, and her heart stopped beating for a couple seconds. There was no way this could be Trina, his so-called "friend" who was with him the night they met at the club. This couldn't be the Trina that Donovan had assured her time and again meant nothing to him romantically. This couldn't be the Trina who wasn't his type.

"*Did you say fianceé?*"

"*Yes, I did. I take it this is Chassidy?*"

"*It is. I'm just a little confused. Donovan told me that the two of you are just friends.*"

"*I'm sure he did,*" *Trina said nonchalantly.* "*I allow him to 'play' when I'm on the road. The night you two met, I encouraged him to talk to you. You seemed like the type he enjoys and I knew I'd be out of town for a few weeks.*"

"*Are you serious? You allow your man to cheat?*

"*I'm on the road A LOT! I allow my man to be satisfied by other women when I'm out doing my thing. We're mature adults. It's what we do. I understand that a man has needs, so I encouraged him to fill them with you until I could get back to fill him up."*

Chassidy was speechless.

Trina continued, "It was obvious what you and your homegirl were there for. Donovan asked me what I thought about you, and I gave him my permission to go for it."

Chassidy thought back to that night and it all made sense. Donovan and Trina did look like more than friends the night at the club, and they had appeared to discuss something kinky involving Chassidy. Now she knew that her gut instinct was right and she felt stupid.

"I never would have talked to him if I had known the two of you were together," *Chassidy said to let Trina know that she in no way intended to violate the girl code.*

"Oh, I know. I could tell that about you, too. That's why I'm telling you this now. A baby would really complicate things for Donovan and me. I already have to come out of my pockets like crazy to support his daughter. Another child by another woman just isn't in my budget right now."

"Daughter?" *Chassidy managed.*

"Donyel. The cute little girl you met at his mother's house."

"That's his daughter?" Chassidy asked.

She thought about how gorgeous Donyel was—come to think of it, she looked just like Donovan. They had the same eyes, dimples, and gap-toothed smile. She wondered if Donyel knew that he was her father. Donovan had seemed so disgusted by Donyel and her mother. What a cold way to treat your very own child. She was happy she had chosen not to bring another of his into the world.

"This is all so sick and twisted."

"Donovan and I tell each other everything. I couldn't stand his stepfather—or his baby momma, or his sister, so I suggested he take you."

"What?" Chassidy asked in disbelief. Her initial hurt had turned to full-on anger. "You suggested he take me? Well, did he tell you about the places he put his tongue on me that day?"

"You need to calm down. I'm not your enemy nor am I trying to make this hurt any more than it has to. But, yes. I know about the park, the repass, lookout hill, the restaurant bathrooms, the movie theatre, the hotels, and all the other places. And *thank you for keeping him busy while I was away. I'm back now."*

"You don't have to worry about me. Donovan and I are as good as done."

There was a long pause. Chassidy looked at her phone to see if Trina was still there.

"Let me school you on what will happen next. In a couple weeks Donovan will call you. When he does, it will be because I am on the road again. He's going to apologize and try to hook up with you again. I will have given him the ok to do that. It's funny how easily men are controlled without them even knowing it. You give them a little freedom and they get confused and look to you to make it all make sense to them. I learned that as a very young woman. Anyway, you decide what happens after that. If you choose to lay with him, please make sure he is covered up and you are on some type of birth control. I'm not trying to end up on an episode of Snapped—and that's not a threat—I'm just saying."

Chassidy was seething. She didn't know exactly how to respond to any of this.

"Are you his pimp or something?"

Trina laughed heartily. "Pimp? That's a good one. A pimp doesn't make an honest man out of her hoe. I'm just an enlightened woman who loves my man and will do anything to keep him happy. If I was his pimp, he would have gotten more out of you than sex and a few free meals in the hood, trust me."

Chassidy was silent.

"Well, I had the abortion, in case you were wondering." As soon as she had said the words, tears streamed down her face as if they were the waters of Niagara Falls.

Trina breathed what sounded like relief. "Oh, good. I didn't want to flat out ask because I know how uncomfortable that can be."

"You have no idea," Chassidy said under her breath.

"Well, I'm gonna let you go now. You can see that I called you from Donovan's number, so don't worry about calling him back. When he's with me he knows not to call other women. When I leave this time I'm going to have his number changed—there were a few other women who ended up being more problematic than we anticipated—restraining order type females. Donovan will call you."

"Please. Ask. Him. To. Lose. My. Number."

Trina chuckled. "Will do, and I look forward to talking with you again soon."

The call ended.

Chassidy looked at her phone but couldn't see much for the tears.

That night, Serenity "read" a story to Chassidy to cheer her up. She also agreed to lay with her and stay awake until Chassidy fell asleep. Within twenty minutes of them hitting the pillow, Serenity was sound asleep, leaving Chassidy alone with thoughts similar to the ones that continued to plague her until this day.

How could I let this happen? she asked herself for the thousandth time. She still couldn't come up with an answer that excused her circumstances.

19

God's Got You

✻ ✻ ✻

Over the course of the next few weeks, things only got worse for Chassidy. She found herself drinking a lot more than her occasional glass of wine. A recreational activity quickly turned into a nightly ritual for her. She found that the only way she could sleep through the night was to free her mind with a bottle of liquid forgetfulness. She started off with shot glasses of tequila blended with mango margarita mix and ice, but after a few nights she dropped the margarita mix and ice and took swigs straight from the bottle.

Some mornings, she woke well after the time she should have been at work because she forgot to set an alarm the night before. The director from Serenity's daycare called a few times to make sure everything was ok. Eric began threatening to take her to court for full custody of Serenity.

After one of Chassidy's drunken "maybe we can work this all out" calls, Eric even threatened to file for full custody that required Chassidy's visits with Serenity to be supervised if she didn't hurry up and get herself together.

On the days she made it to work, she could tell that Sam no longer viewed her with the same respect she had for so many years prior.

It all hurt so badly.

One day as she sat in her office and stared out the window, Kim and Sam both pushed through her door and Sam closed it behind them.

"What are you doing here?" Chassidy asked.

"You haven't answered any of my calls, so I figured I would try my luck here."

"I'm fine...really," Chassidy lied.

"No you're not," Sam said. "Even the Mr. Baxter has started to whisper about you needing to take some permanent time off. It's getting harder to cover for you when your lack of focus and drive are so apparent. You're obviously hung over when you do actually make it in."

"Look!" Kim said, "You have got to pull yourself together. If you can't do it for yourself, you need to do it for Serenity. That little girl worships the ground you walk on and her trifling daddy is just waiting to jump on the opportunity to keep her away from you. Trust me...that's not what you want."

Chassidy looked out the window. She didn't respond.

"I was thinking," Sam said, "My cousin, Sharon, is a Christian therapist. I kinda mentioned to her some of the things you've been dealing with and she suggested you take some time off and work with her for a couple weeks."

"I'm not crazy," Chassidy said indignantly. "I don't need to see a therapist."

This time, Kim took over. "No one said you're crazy, Chas. That's the problem with black folk. We think that seeing someone to help us work through our problems makes us weak—or crazy. White folk, on the other hand, know that therapists are the key to optimal mental health and start seeing them when they're still in diapers. You probably don't know this, but I have been seeing a therapist for the past year. I got so depressed after Lemural and I broke up that I thought about committing suicide."

"What?" Chassidy said. "You never told me that."

"I was embarrassed. When he left I realized that he was never really into me as much as I was into him. That's what hurt the most. My therapist has really helped me get to the root of why I was so prone to seeking out and participating in toxic relationships."

"Suicide?" The thought of Kim, who Chassidy always said was the strongest woman she knew, contemplating taking her life over a failed relationship with Lemural was just too much for Chassidy to bear. "Why didn't you talk to me, Kim? I'm your best friend."

"Probably for the same reason you've been ignoring my calls even though I'm *your* best friend."

Chassidy thought about it and nodded her head. The tears she had been struggling to keep from falling all day finally won the battle and streamed down her face.

Kim leaned down and gave her a hug.

"I understand, Chas. I really do. But you're strong! You are going to come through all of this so much stronger. You're going to see just how worthy you are."

Chassidy let out a primal moan. The tears refused to stop.

"My cousin has helped quite a few people get through situations like yours," Sam said. "You can Google her and see that she's the truth—a strong woman of God with a conviction to help broken people find the healing they need in the only One who can fully mend you. Her clients are always pleased with their results. If you'd like, I can give her a call and get the ball rolling today."

"I need to think about it."

"Boss lady, trust me. You are out of time if you don't do this. You need to decide today, right now. I will walk out of this office and let the Mr. Baxter know that you do still want this job and just need to take a short leave of absence. But if I don't, I can guarantee you'll have walking papers by the end of the week."

Chassidy was surprised to hear how close she was to losing her job. Considering how much of an asset she was to the company, she knew that things must be really bad if the president of the bank was willing to let her go. Chassidy needed this job, especially with all the new bills that came along with being single. Losing this job would force her to tap into her savings and if nothing else came up, she would be completely broke before long. Being unemployed wasn't an option.

"Serenity needs you to be at your best, Chassidy. She needs to see that even though life hurts sometimes, we are strong women who face challenges head on. She needs to see what it looks like to claim victory and get back up after a fall. She's young, but she's smart, and she sees you. She may forget the tiny details of the past few weeks, but she will never forget the strength and the resilience you exhibited because of it. It will be etched in her mind forever, and she will be a stronger woman because of it. But you have to choose now. What will Serenity see?" Kim asked.

Another sob. "She's already seen so much dysfunction. My God!" Chassidy cried.

"What will she see next?" Kim asked.

Chassidy looked at Sam, whose eyes oozed a love and concern like Chassidy had never seen in her before. "Please give your cousin a call."

Sam smiled, nodded, and gave Chassidy a hug. "It really will be alright," she assured her. "God's got you."

20

Stronger

✳ ✳ ✳

Chassidy lost track of time. Sometimes it felt like time was standing still and other times it felt like it was moving too quickly. One thing she knew was that although it felt like it had been an eternity since she had seen Donovan's face, according to her phone's calendar it had actually only been three months. The first month had been hell.

The second, purgatory.

The last, the emotional doldrums. The thought of all she had been through still hurt, but at least things were slowly getting better. She looked forward to the day she would smile from her heart.

Before meeting Dr. Sharon, Chassidy decided that she wouldn't mention Donovan or the abortion, or Trina or Donyel. She would keep that really ugly stuff to herself and just talk about the struggles brought on by her failed marriage.

When she met Dr. Sharon face to face, her plan quickly changed. Being in her presence, Chassidy was keenly aware that what Sam told her about Dr. Sharon was true. She was a woman of God with a conviction to help broken hearts.

Chassidy felt peace. She felt like Dr. Sharon was someone she could talk to without fear of being judged. That made all the difference in the world.

They were supposed to talk for 45 minutes on their first meeting, but the session went on for two hours. During that time, Chassidy bared her soul and she felt a huge weight lift because of it. She was surprised by how easy it was to talk to Dr. Sharon.

They determined that they should probably start off with two hour sessions for the first few months and make adjustments as time passed.

The sessions brought up a lot of issues Chassidy had never properly dealt with. She realized that she had deep abandonment issues that developed when her father left as a child. They also uncovered that Chassidy had a great deal of animosity toward her mother because she blamed her for getting involved with a man like her father.

Through their sessions, Chassidy also came to realize that she was disappointed in herself for falling into the same unhealthy relationship patterns that she had learned from her mother.

To top it all off, she was upset with God for His role in all of it. He could have prevented the bad stuff if he had wanted to. He could remove her current pain in an instant if He wanted to.

She hated that the things she hoped to protect Serenity from were the very things that Serenity had already witnessed too much of.

One of the key areas of their sessions was forgiveness. Dr. Sharon constantly gave Chassidy scriptures to read and exercises to do regarding forgiveness. In order for her to completely heal, Chassidy would have to forgive her mother, her father, Eric, Trina, Donovan, and all the other people who had hurt her.

Most importantly, she would have to forgive herself and God. Forgiving them would free her, according to Dr. Sharon.

Dr. Sharon promised that freedom in Christ would change her life.

Chassidy desired that freedom.

As she sat on her couch and worked on the assignment Dr. Sharon had given her after their session that day, she heard the toilet flush.

"Are you alright, baby?" she yelled to Serenity.

Instead of answering, Serenity soon joined her mother in the living room.

"Sit on my lap," Chassidy said as she lifted Serenity. "What are you doing up? Did you have another bad dream?"

Serenity shook her head.

"Can I sleep with you tonight?" she asked as she batted her tired eyes.

Chassidy looked at the clock. It was almost midnight.

"Of course you can, baby girl. Go lay in my bed, and I'll be in there in a sec, okay?"

"Ok, Mommy," Serenity said as she dragged her feet toward her mother's room. Chassidy thanked

God for blessing her with the perfect daughter. It was as if she was wise beyond her years. Chassidy was keenly aware that her daughter didn't think she was perfect, but she could tell that her imperfections didn't make Serenity love her any less.

Serenity always seemed to know what to say and when to say it, and her request to sleep with Chassidy was her way of letting her mother know that it was way past both of their bedtimes. Chassidy smiled and wrote that in her journal.

Just as she reached for the remote, a notification appeared on the screen of her phone. It was a text from an unknown phone number. She opened the message.

Unknown: *Hi. It's Donovan. This is my new number. I'm sorry. I miss you and I really want to get together so we can talk about everything. I love you, Chas, and I swear I never meant to hurt you.*

Chassidy thought back to her conversation with Trina.

"Let me school you on what will happen next. In a couple weeks Donovan will call you. When he does, it will be because I am on the road again. He's going to apologize and try to hook up with you

again. I will have given him the ok to do that. It's funny how easily men are controlled without them even knowing it. You give them a little freedom and they get confused and look to you to make it all make sense to them. I learned that as a very young woman. Anyway, you decide what happens after that. If you choose to lay with him, please make sure he is covered up and you are on some type of birth control. I'm not trying to end up on an episode of Snapped—and that's not a threat—I'm just saying."

This text had come a little later than Chassidy anticipated, but she was glad it had because she was stronger now than she would have been two months ago.

She would not play second to another woman ever again.

Donovan was fine, but he was emotionally unavailable. He was immature. He was not playing an active role in his beautiful daughter's life. Giving time or attention to him would only cause the cycle of dysfunction to continue. Chassidy was growing to believe that she deserved better.

Another text came through.

Unknown number: *Look. I'm not too far from your house right now. Maybe I can stop by and we can talk. I really just want to talk and explain everything to you. I'm sure you were led to believe some things about me that aren't true. At least give me a chance to tell you my side.*

He followed up the text with a photograph of himself making a silly face.

Another text followed:

Unknown number: *I'm sorry. I hope you can forgive me.*

Seeing his picture sent a chill through Chassidy's body. She remembered all the sensations she had felt whenever he touched her. Oh, how she longed to be touched. Would it really hurt to respond to his text?

At that moment Psalm 27:14 came to mind. "Wait for the Lord. Be strong and take heart and wait for the Lord."

How long would she have to wait?

She could send Donovan a text and let him know that she had forgiven him and ask him to lose her number. Wouldn't she want someone to give her the same respect? She countered that thought with a reminder that she never would have done to anyone in the first place what Donovan had done to her.

Then, Proverbs 3:5-6 came to mind. "Trust in the Lord with all your heart and lean not unto your own understanding. In all your ways acknowledge Him and He shall direct your paths."

She sensed strongly in her spirit that responding to him would be akin to Eve responding to the serpent in the Garden of Eden.

But she was so lonely. At least if she did indulge Donovan she would be well aware of what she was getting into. She could just "play" with him as well, right?

Philippians 4:13 came to mind. This time she said aloud, "I can do all things through Christ which strengthens me."

All things meant that she could live life without Donovan. She could live life without Eric. She could live life without anyone who didn't recognize her as the royal priesthood—the queen—that God created her to be. It would be hard, but she could do it.

She looked at her messages from Donovan one last time before she deleted them and blocked his number. If he reached out in other ways, Chassidy would continue to use the tools Dr. Sharon had shared to help her through tempting situations. She would fight with the word of God.

She flicked off the television and headed to her room. She scooted Serenity over a little and laid next to her beautiful baby girl. She closed her eyes and prayed:

God, I'm sorry for my lack of faith. I thank You for being faithful. Thank You for Your unconditional love. Thank You for Your forgiveness. I'm sorry I ever blamed You for the messes I made. Thank You for keeping me. Thank You for protecting me. Thank You for working all things together for my good. Thank You for revealing truth to me. Thank You for being patient with me. Thank You for holding my hand as I walk through one of the most difficult times of my life. Thank You for removing toxic people from my life. Thank You for my friends and family who have kept me lifted up in prayer. Thank You for my beautiful daughter. Thank You for helping me to set a good example for her. I thank You for being true love in our lives.

I remember praying a while back that You would send me a man who would love me like You do. I got confused along the way. But now I see that you wanted to be the number one desire of my heart. And You are, God! I want You, God. I need you, God. I love you, God!

Acknowledgements

I would like to thank my daughter, Khyra, (the Love of My Life) for being my biggest cheerleader. Since she was a little girl, she has always said, "You can do it, Mommy!"

I would like to thank all of my nieces (my Heartbeats) for being so loving and supportive. They always have my back.

To my sister in law, Lillie and my aunt Thomasina: Thank you for being there when I needed you.

I want to thank my cousin Tabitha (Tab) for always seeing in me what I did not see in myself.

To Letisha (Tish), my prayer partner, thanks for speaking life into me and building me up. I believe the dreams you have had about me are now coming true.

To Joi, Lynda, and Latressa (Tree): Thank you for being great friends through everything.

To my cousin, Talisha (Tee): Thanks for being my right hand.

To Minister Campbell: Thank you for your love, support and prayers.

To my New Beginnings Church family, Pastor Michael Ellerbe and Lady Ellerbe: Thank you for being great spiritual parents. I am so blessed to have you as my covering.

A huge thanks to all of my readers and supporters.

51880213R10109

Made in the USA
Columbia, SC
27 February 2019